# Dancing in the Rain

Also by Marie Trotignon

And He Shall Be Called Nicholas

The Dance of the Blue Crab

# Dancing in the Rain

*A Collection of Raindrops and Rainbows*

## Marie Trotignon

iUniverse, Inc.
Bloomington

# Dancing in the Rain
## A Collection of Raindrops and Rainbows

iUniverse books may be ordered through booksellers or by contacting:

iUniverse
1663 Liberty Drive
Bloomington, IN 47403
www.iuniverse.com
1-800-Authors (1-800-288-4677)

Because of the dynamic nature of the Internet, any Web addresses or links contained in this book may have changed since publication and may no longer be valid. The views expressed in this work are solely those of the author and do not necessarily reflect the views of the publisher, and the publisher hereby disclaims any responsibility for them.

Any people depicted in stock imagery provided by Thinkstock are models, and such images are being used for illustrative purposes only.

Certain stock imagery © Thinkstock.

ISBN: 978-1-4502-7904-8 (sc)
ISBN: 978-1-4502-7906-2 (dj)
ISBN: 978-1-4502-7905-5 (ebk)

Printed in the United States of America

iUniverse rev. date: 11/29/2010

To those whose love and encouragement
taught me to dance in the rain

# Acknowledgements

There are so many names that should appear here: My mother and father with their intuitive understanding of the needs of a dreamer, my sister and brother with their steadfast approval of the fruits of my imagination, the Creative Writing instructors assisting me along the literary pathway, the many friends and fellow aspiring authors with their staunch support of my efforts, the Seahurst Writers keeping me focused, and finally, Harry McIntyre, whose faith in my writing skills encouraged me to publish—my thanks to you all.

# INTRODUCTION

The intriguing world of fantasy and fiction has always held a fascination for me. Even as I child, I was a dreamer, a castle builder, making up my own bedtime story each night, the theme of which, ultimately interrupted by sleep, could often continue for weeks. As an adult dealing with the vacillating realities of life, transcribing my ventures into the fanciful became my passion; a refuge, a catharsis; an outlet of flights into my imagination.

I would share with you this collection of raindrops and rainbows, gathered over the years. In order to give some semblance and chronicled order to these offerings, I have preceded each grouping of compositions with a poem or bit of prose, hoping to set the tone or mood for that which follows.

I invite you, now, to join me as I dance in the rain.

# Contents

# TODAY'S FORECAST:
# WARM AND SUNNY

# MUSHROOMS

Mushrooms, she said
Picked fresh today.
Served in an omelette.
You'll like them that way.

I'll have to admit,
They went down rather easy.
But now I discover,
My stomach's a bit queasy.

My eyes will not focus,
My head's in a spin.
My knees have grown weak,
The air has grown thin.

My body is chilled,
I shiver with cold.
My forehead is damp,
And clammy as mold.

I need to lie down.
I turn toward my bed.
But find in its place,
A giant turtle instead.

I throw open the window
And recoil in surprise.
For staring at me,
Are hundreds of eyes.

Above in the heavens
Hangs a big yellow moon.
Shining so brightly,
The night is like noon.

Then I spy the blue heron
Swooping down from the sky.
With huge flapping wings
It fills the night with its cry.

The creature draws nearer
I am fraught with dismay.
For its silvery beard,
Has become hair . . . that is gray.

There's a long pointed nose
Where once its beak grew,
And each grayish webbed foot
Wears a red pointed shoe.

My heart is now pounding
With the awareness this brings.
Instead of a blue heron,
It's an old woman . . . with wings!

My poor head is aching,
Bells ring in my ears.
I sink to the floor,
Overcome by my fears.

It's a bright morning sun
Beating warm on my face
That awakens me to find,
Everything in its place.

I vow at that moment,
Never more to consume,
Any questionable fungi
That's called a mushroom.

# THE ELEPHANT AND THE BLINDMEN

"Today, all day, the air has smelled of snow."

In the silence that followed, I could sense their denial even before I saw it in their faces. Eyes lowered, expressions guarded, they fidgeted restlessly. I knew what was coming and I felt my stomach tightening into its pre-Mylanta knot. Why was it always this way? Why did they have to challenge my every observation, question my every comment, dissect and tear apart my every idea?

It was John who spoke first, as I knew it would be. He would defy even the Pope. "Well, now, I don't think I've ever heard that one before." I felt the muscles in my jaw tighten at the derision in his voice. "You can't smell snow. It might *feel* like snow, but you don't *smell* snow."

"Really, John?" The smile I forced to my lips felt tight. "And just how would you say snow "feels"?

"Well, you can just feel it. It's in the air. Maybe it's the humidity, or the temperature. I don't know. But I can feel it in the air when it's going to snow."

"I disagree with you, John." That was Ed now, always quick to join the conflict once the first jab of criticism had been delivered. "I think you can *hear* an impending snowstorm."

"Hear snow?" I snorted. I made no effort to hide the irritation gathering behind my eyes and now throbbing at my temples. "Come on, Ed. Get real."

"No," he insisted. "It's true. Haven't you noticed how quiet it is just before it snows? No birds . . . right? Except for maybe a seagull or two headed inland. And *all* sound is muffled, like you're, maybe, inside a cotton ball."

"That's a hurricane, Ed." It didn't surprise me that Charlie's quip earned him nothing more than a belligerent scowl.

"You can *see* the snow coming." I turned in surprise at the sound of Kathy's soft voice. She usually didn't get involved in these bashing sessions. I saw her face redden as all eyes turned toward her. "The clouds are different," she continued bravely. "Not like rain clouds that are gray, or even black. Snow clouds look kind of like dingy white sheets, and they sort of hunker down, close to the earth, until there is no horizon. It's like . . . like sitting in the middle of a big white cloud."

"Cripes! You'd better stick to art critiquing, Kathy." This sharp rebuke came from George.

I caught the apologetic glance Kathy sent my way and winked my forgiveness at her while silently cursing George for his insensitivity.

"I can *taste* the coming snow," George went on, totally oblivious to the raised eyebrows in the room "I remember when I was a kid, I used to catch snowflakes on my tongue. I remember thinking they tasted like metal. Even now, before it snows, I get this metallic taste in my mouth. Never fails. I always know when it's going to snow."

"Probably got his tongue stuck to a flagpole when he was a kid." John's sarcasm surfaced again.

"Hey, you guys. This is beginning to turn into a pretty flaky conference." Charlie's effort to lighten the tension came too late. I could feel anger crowding into my chest, cramping the muscles in my neck.

"Think what you like!" All at once, I was tired of the endless bickering. "I can *smell* snow in the air," I snapped. "And I'm willing to bet any person in this room we're due for a snowstorm. Let's see . . . today is Tuesday, I'll lay you ten-to-one odds we see snow no later than Thursday."

"You're on!"

I swung toward the voice coming from the back of the room. In the shadows, I could see a technician frantically waving his arms. Suddenly, the adrenaline was pumping, and, like melting snow, I felt the tension slip from my shoulders. I shot a warning glance around the table. Then, taking a deep breath, I turned, and smiled into the camera.

"And now, for tonight's weather forecast."

# THE CHALLENGE

I tried to concentrate on the beauty of the landscape as it swept past me, tried to focus my eyes upon the pristine blanket of snow covering the earth; the tree branches drooping beneath their heavy burden of frozen rain. But with a magnetic–like morbid fascination, my gaze was drawn back to that little white patch of ground dropping swiftly away beneath my feet.

My heart stumbled and I knew a moment of overwhelming panic. What was I doing here perched in a swaying metal chair, two narrow boards strapped to my feet, dangling precariously from a quite probably inadequate steel cable as it creaked its way up a dangerously steep mountainside? It had been nearly fifteen years since I had schussed down the groomed slopes of a western Washington ski resort. It had once been one of the greatest joys of my life. But, that was a long time ago. Would it be like riding a bicycle, I wondered? Would it all come back to me? Or would I spend the next six months with various parts of my body encased in white plaster cocoons?

My heart tripped, then raced forward as I forced my gaze toward the approaching crest of the hill where the chair lift ended. The moment was near when I would need to thrust my poles into the frozen snow and propel myself forward, leaving the empty chair to execute its U-turn around the giant greasy hub before wobbling its way back to the base of the hill.

Nervously, I readied my skis, tightened my mitten-clad hands about the pole grips. Now! Now! Thrust! Push! I cringed as the sound of grinding gears splintered the frigid mountain air. The cable clanged menacingly against its metal casing and the chair lift shuddered to a stop. When I'd finally summoned the courage to open my eyes, I was relieved to discover the problem was not a mechanical one. My chair had successfully maneuvered its U-turn and was poised in readiness for its downward journey. The problem, unfortunately, was me. Mentally, I had skillfully ejected myself from the metal chair and onto the slopes. Physically, I still cowered in the comparative safety of the chair's cold, impersonal embrace.

A young ski lift operator in a bright orange jumpsuit emerged from the glassed-in control booth and approached me from behind, that being his only directional option. "Stay where you are, Ma'am," he pleaded needlessly. "I'll have to help you down."

Positioning himself beneath my dangling feet, my rescuer first pried the poles from my hands, then, lifting his arms, grabbed me about the waist and wrestled me from my perch. I learned, during that eternity of embarrassment, there is no graceful way to exit a chair lift once it has passed the designated point of debarkation. Carefully balancing me on my skis, the young man planted the poles once again in my grasp, pointed me down-hill and gave me a gentle shove. I slithered down the slope in a stinging cloud of total humiliation.

For the second time, I swung above the snow-covered hillside, my derriere firmly pressed to the curved back of a swaying lift chair. I'd convinced myself that, like riding a bike, or a horse, if I didn't get right back on after a spill, I'd never find the courage to do so. Up ahead, the lift shack crouched like an ugly blister atop the hill. As we neared the scene of my earlier degradation, I could make out the orange jumper of the attendant and knew he had also spotted me. I could only guess at the disturbing thoughts playing havoc with his mind.

Gritting my teeth in determination, I gripped my poles and lifted the tips of my skis. Leaning anxiously forward, I was prepared to hurl myself into space when, just before the point of my self-launch, the chair lift jolted to a stop. Flashing me a condescending smile, my self-appointed guardian waited patiently until I stood and clumsily pushed myself out of its way before allowing the chair to continue on. This time, wary skiers moved obligingly aside as I plowed my disgruntled way to the bottom of the hill.

Once again, I stood in line, waiting for the metal chair to nudge the back of my knees before sweeping me off my feet. Once again, my dreaded nemesis hove into view. Once again, I saw the orange-clad figure hovering over the control panel. I lifted one ski pole to capture his attention, waving it wildly in the air while shaking my head vigorously back and forth. The young man hesitated, then slowly, uncertainly, withdrew his hand from the lever that would halt the chair lift's forward motion. I was parallel with him now, could see the concern clouding his boyish face.

Once again, I tightened the grip on my poles, positioned my skies and then . . . I thrust! I pushed! And miracle of miracles, I was up and away, careening around the loop to the opposite side of the control-booth, my skis eagerly gripping the slope's grooved track. The young attendant ran from his post, hands raised above his head in a thumbs-up salute. His shouts of "Hooray, you did it" followed me down the hill.

The cold wind covers my face with its boisterous kisses. The snow chatters excitedly beneath my skis. My heart, drunk with adrenaline, leaps wildly within me. Never has the freedom of a run been so exhilarating. Today, the mountain is my kingdom! No matter that I'm the master of none. Today, I have mastered the bunny slope chair lift!

# THE VALENTINE CAPER

*How could I have been so stupid*? I fought an urge to beat my head against the hard stucco wall outside Apartment 4B.

The minute the envelope left my fingers, I knew I had committed the most asinine act of my life. This morning's beautiful brainchild, conceived as a lark, had transmuted itself into a demonic urchin, threatening me with total humiliation.

Finding myself "between boyfriends" again, I was absolutely delighted when a devastatingly handsome young man moved into the apartment next to mine shortly after Christmas. Broad muscular shoulders straining against the confinement of his sports jacket suggested he was a frequent visitor at the local gym. This, along with a pair of sensual brown eyes twinkling beneath a crown of crisp, dark curls, prompted me, privately, of course, to label my new neighbor, "Big Hunk." Our polite "good mornings" in the hallway had advanced to good-natured bantering as our schedules found us sharing the elevator twice a day. Resigned to my rather "plain Jane" attributes, I was ordinarily not the aggressive type, but must admit, on occasion, I purposely delayed my morning departure to coincide with his.

So, when I glanced at the calendar this morning and discovered it was February 14th, I rationalized it would only be a neighborly gesture should I give "Big Hunk" a valentine . . . it was, after all, just in fun.

When no one answered the doorbell, I assumed my neighbor was working late and blithely slid the incriminating missile under the door. At that exact moment, the awful possible consequences of my action overwhelmed me. Somewhat tardily, it occurred to me, instead of being late, he might be out on a date, might conceivably bring his girlfriend back to the apartment. I cringed at the thought. I *must* get that valentine back!

My frantic brain grasped at straws. Maybe I could fish it out the same way I'd slipped it in. Dropping to my hands and knees, I pressed my face against the rough weave of the Berber carpet, cursing the conscientious architect who designed the building's draft-free construction. I could barely see the crimson edge of the coveted envelope, but there was no room for my probing fingers to invade that snug fit between door and carpeting.

A slight vibration of the floorboards interrupted my concentration. Uncomfortably aware of my compromising position, ear to the carpet, posterior looming above my shoulders like some gigantic Mt. Vesuvius, I carefully turned my head until my eyes rested upon a pair of sturdy brown oxfords. Slowly, my gaze traveled up a pair of stocking-clad legs, swung from the coarse hem of a tweed skirt, rappelled across an ample, sweater-clothed bosom and onto the scowling countenance of Mrs. Olsen, tenant in Apartment 4D.

Attempting an explanation seemed rather pointless. Rising regally to my feet, I carefully smoothed my sweater over my hips. "Have a nice day," I smiled sweetly. Gathering the remnants of my dignity about me, I quickly retreated down the hallway.

Inside my apartment, I agonized over my predicament. I had no qualms about Mrs. Olsen's opinion of me. My concern at this moment was the imminent arrival of Big Hunk and his girlfriend. I had to gain access to his apartment, by whatever means. And since there was no legal way of doing so, it seemed I would have to resort to burglary. I sifted through the chaff of my memory banks, trying to recall the crime mysteries I'd read, the shady characters skulking across my television screen.

*Wait*! An idea snagged itself in my sieve-like memory. *What about the old credit card maneuver?* The hard square of plastic slipped inside the doorframe is supposed to flatten the latch so the door can be easily opened. My desperate brain deemed it worthy of a try. Emptying my purse onto the bed, I pawed through its contents until my hand closed about the sharp edges of my credit card.

Quietly opening the portal to my apartment, I peered cautiously into the hallway, then slipped down the corridor to Apartment 4B. Reaffirming I was alone, I carefully slid the rigid plastic into the crevice between the door and it frame. Once again, I cursed the builder's fetish for tight-fitting doors. I laboriously inched my makeshift key into the inadequate opening, wriggling it, pressing it inward. I listened in hopeful anticipation for the gentle click of a released latch, but heard, instead, the brittle snap of a broken credit card. I stared at the plastic remnant in my hand, realizing the half with my name on it was trapped in the doorjamb. This time, I made no effort to control the urge. With considerable enthusiasm, I whacked my head against the grainy plaster of the wall.

The unmistakable creak of a door hinge interrupted my self-abuse. I looked up to find myself gazing into one accusing eyeball, glaring at me through the cracked doorway of Apartment 4D. The door quickly closed, and my stomach did a flip-flop as I imagined Mrs. Olsen at her phone, dialing the number of the building superintendent.

*The building superintendent . . . of course! Why hadn't I thought of him sooner? I'll call the superintendent, tell him I smell smoke coming from Apartment 4B. When he opens the door, I'll grab the valentine, the other half of my credit card, and no one will be the wiser. The perfect solution*!

I hurried back to my apartment and snatching up the phone, jabbed in the code that would connect me with Mr. Peterson. The irritating buzz piped into my ear confirmed my suspicions Mrs. Olsen had wasted no time. I broke the connection, then impatiently pressed Mr. Peterson's buttons again. This time, the superintendent's gravelly voice came over the wire. Hastily, I poured out my contrived fears, listening gleefully as Mr. Peterson reluctantly agreed to meet me with the passkey.

I had nearly worn a groove in the carpeting with my restless pacing before the jangle of keys heralded the approach of my unsuspecting accomplice.

"Hurry, Mr. Peterson," I urged, all but dragging him down the hallway.

Ignoring my state of near-hysteria, my unwitting partner-in-crime paused outside Apartment 4B, hunched close to its paneled portal, his bulbous nose wriggling as he sniffed the air.

"I dunno," he pondered. "I don't smell nothin'." His rheumy eyes narrowed. "I ain't supposed to go into these apartments 'less it's an emergency."

"Oh, but this *is* an emergency," I insisted. "I've been smelling smoke all afternoon."

"Well . . ." His fingers dug thoughtfully at his scalp. "Miz Olsen did say she seen you snooping around the hallway."

"There! See!" I crowed, secretly reveling in this unexpected turn-about. I struggled against an overpowering impulse to wrench the key ring from Mr. Peterson's hand as, groping among the tangled collection at his belt, he finally selected one notched piece of metal and inserted it into the lock.

At long last, the door snapped open. I lunged forward, snatching a tumbling, mutilated bit of plastic from midair. I turned then, toward the purpose of my venture into crime, only to find that object skewered to the floor by the size eleven shoe of the superintendent, now fumbling to remove the stubborn key from the lock.

"Hello, is something wrong?"

At the sound of that familiar voice, my heart contemplated early retirement. Reluctantly, I turned to face Big Hunk, noting, with relief, he was alone.

"Oh, hi." My voice struggled its way across the dry Sahara of my throat. "I . . . I thought I smelled smoke. That is . . ."

Brushing me aside, Big Hunk hurried into his apartment. I heard him moving through the rooms; then he was standing before us again, apparently satisfied with his inspection.

"Everything seems to be okay," he assured us with his to-die-for smile.

"I . . . I'm glad," I stammered. But my attention was riveted to the red envelope, freed from imprisonment as Mr. Peterson returned to the hallway. Cautiously, I edged towards my objective.

"Well, what have we here?"

I could only hope a giant meteor would crash into the building, as Big Hunk stooped to retrieve the envelope.

Like a predatory vulture, my hand swooped to snatch it from his fingers. "Oh, that's mine." I barely recognized the falsetto squeak that escaped my lips. "I must have dropped it."

Big Hunk stared at me, a quizzical look upon his face. Mr. Peterson shuffled off toward the elevators, muttering to himself about nosey, busybody tenants. I had no doubt Mrs. Olsen was peering through the cracked doorway of Apartment 4D. I wanted nothing more than to return to the womb-like security of my own apartment.

"Thanks. I really appreciate your concern."

Guilt warmed my face at the gratitude in Big Hunk's husky, mesmerizing voice.

"I feel I owe you." A twinkle of amusement now danced in those sensuous brown eyes. "What say we go out and grab a bite to eat . . . sort of celebrate?"

"Celebrate?" I parroted weakly.

"For one thing, my apartment isn't on fire. And, well," he glanced meaningfully at the scarlet envelope clutched in my hand. "After all, this *is* Valentine's Day."

# DON'T FEED THE KITTY

By nature, I am not a cat person. I've never been a cat owner, though I'm told this is a misnomer— no one ever owns a cat. Better to say my association with the feline population has been limited. We shared our lives with cats when I was a youngster living on the ranch, but they were not pets. They were outdoor cats, *hit-men*, (or *hit-cats* if you would have it so), earning their keep by ridding the barn and outbuildings of pesky, grain-eating rodents.

The only cat I recall ever being allowed in the house was a stray appearing at our back door one cold, blustery night in early October. Mother took pity upon the poor hungry, bedraggled creature and took her in, feeding and warming her by the fire. That cat remained with us during the entire winter, regally ensconced in her warm bed beside the kitchen stove, disdainfully rejecting overtures from anyone but my mother.

Fat and sassy come spring, our house guest left one morning by the same back door through which she'd entered, and did not return . . . until late fall when ominous snow clouds hovered impatiently upon the mountain's crest. This winter/summer arrangement continued for as many years as I can remember, Mother accepting this part-time pet on its own terms. I however, chose to ignore this haughty panhandler, as she ignored me. Perhaps that explains my feeling, or lack of feeling, for the feline species. By nature, or by necessity, we are both stubbornly independent.

My second experience with one of these shameless exploiters came last year after my dog, my erstwhile companion of fifteen years, left for more hallowed pastures. Shortly thereafter, the neighbor's twenty-year-old cat, Misha, noting the absence of canine interference, began appearing outside my dining room door. She was rather a scraggly looking thing so, out of pity and compassion, one warm day I foolishly offered her a dish of cool milk.

Major mistake! Thereafter, each morning's breakfast hour found her demanding her daily handout. She had a voice difficult to ignore, husky and gravelly like that of an aging barfly who spent too many hours sucking on cigarettes and sipping cheap whiskey. If I happened to be slow in responding to her demands, Misha would turn her attention to my screen door, methodically shredding it with her sharp, destructive claws. Soon learning there was no undoing this distressing turn of events, I continued the daily dole until, rewarding my act of kindness, poor Misha crawled beneath my house and died. It cost $150.00 for the Odor Control Man to locate and remove the source.

I was pet-free for several months before, realizing I was once again vulnerable, a second neighbor cat appeared in my yard. However, this was not just another stubborn, independent cat. This was a cat with a plan, a plan to invade and conquer. I have no idea if this cat was male or female, only that this was a cat with an *Attitude*.

Our first confrontation came one warm day when I'd opened my back door to let in the fresh spring air. "Cat", as I have dubbed it for sake of identification, accepted this open portal as a personal invitation and blithely followed me down the hallway. My explosive reaction to this intrusion failed to inspire the hasty retreat I expected. Instead, Cat merely turned around and, waving a stiffened tail like a flag of defiance over an arched back, stalked indignantly out the door.

Cat's second invasion proved more successful. It was late afternoon when, carrying a supply of fresh linens, I climbed the stairs to my bedroom. Arms still full, I moved to the nightstand to answer the ringing telephone. In one harrowing second, my quiet afternoon erupted into chaos as Cat lunged from beneath my bed, slithered between my legs and, claws digging into my Persian carpet, skittered across the room and escaped down the stairway.

War had now been declared. The back door was left open only if I was stationed upon the porch. Cat would saunter nonchalantly by, the epitome of indifference, only to, once opposite the open doorway, suddenly leap onto the steps, streak past me and into the house. I soon learned to anticipate my adversary and managed to thwart these surprise attacks. So Cat changed its Modus Opperendi, now lying seemingly docile in the yard's far corner. The moment I became so careless as to venture from my post, Cat was on its feet, hurtling toward a coup. I've developed agility quite remarkable for a lady of my maturity and have succeeded, so far, in heading off this interloper. On the other hand, my opponent was not one to accept defeat graciously. Nose thrust haughtily into the air, Cat would reluctantly retreat to the corner of the yard, arrogantly imitating that insolent, shoulder-rolling gait of defiant street hoodlums I see swaggering across my television screen.

By now, Cat was aware I'm not an easy pushover; that I have become an adversary to be reckoned with. Yet, at this writing, Cat has taken over my yard, soaking up the sun's rays from the comfort of my chaise lounge, lolling at night upon my cushioned patio chairs, all the while, I'm sure, plotting, planning, awaiting my next unguarded moment. Only this morning, when I stepped out to fetch the newspaper, I discovered the mutilated body of a dead mouse upon my doorstep. A gift of surrender, I wondered, or flagrant braggadocio, intended as a warning?

Very well, then, Cat, I accept your challenge. Let the Games begin!

# WILBUR PEABODY, PRIVATE EYE

The man's tall, lanky frame moved easily along the path edging the blue lupine covered field, his dark eyes drinking in the tranquility of the autumn countryside. A warm evening breeze, playing among the long blades of meadow grass, gently stirred a tuft of gray at his feet. He hesitated then bent to examine what appeared to be the abandoned prey of a hungry hawk. Idly curious, he picked up a dry twig and lifted the body of a hapless squirrel from the dust. Oddly, there was no blood on the soft, furry body. Its head, twisted at a grotesque angle, hung limply from a broken neck.

The man's searching gaze probed the grassy area surrounding his grim discovery. Rising to his feet, he cautiously approached a clump of brown feathers lying but a few feet away. With the toe of his sneaker, he nudged the still-warm carcass of a hawk. Once again, there was no outward sign of trauma to the body except . . .. A cold lump of foreboding knotted itself in the man's chest. The bird's neck was broken.

The man glanced uneasily about him, his gaze darting to a nearby clump of cedar trees, huddled like frightened witnesses, their secret but a soft whisper among their branches. The man held his breath, listening. He heard nothing. He peered anxiously toward the shadowy undergrowth. He saw nothing. Yet, he could feel it, in the prickling of hairs stirring at the base of his neck. Some one, some thing, was out there, watching . . . waiting. The man's jaw tightened convulsively, and he ran his tongue over suddenly dry lips. Dark eyes narrowed, he squinted into the sun momentarily poised on the lip of the horizon. An involuntary chill shuddered across the man's shoulders. Quickly he turned back toward the way he had come, eager to retrace his steps.

Without warning, he felt a stunning blow to the back of his head. Strangely, he felt no pain, heard only the sound of bones, snapping in his neck, and then . . . nothing.

The tall, voiceless cedars cast their long shadows across the silent field where now, three still forms lay crumpled beside the path.

+          +          +

"Okay, loser. This the end of the line for you."

His eyes no more than hard, cold slits, Wilbur lifted the corner of his lip in a contemptuous curl. Across the kitchen table, his "Mickey Spillane" reflection sneered back at him from the mirror propped against four empty tuna fish cans. His fingers caressing the dog-eared paperback on the table beside him, Wilbur gazed wistfully at the rugged, slouch-hatted detective boldly eyeing him from the book's glossy cover.

Like green slime, envy oozed through Wilbur's veins. What wouldn't he give to lead the exciting, adventurous life of a private detective? Instead, he was trapped in a dead-end job, sorting mail in the back room of the Morristown postal sub station.

Exchanging his fork for a spoon, Wilbur scraped the last glob of coagulated gravy from the bottom of the aluminum tray housing *Farmer Smith's Heat and Eat Biscuits and Gravy*. On the palette of his imagination, unfettered fantasy painted an image of "Wilbur the Private Eye", complete with brimmed hat and turned up coat collar. How hard could it be, anyway, to become a private detective, he fretted? He'd read every paperback copy of the *Micky Spillane* series, hadn't missed a single episode of Howard Duff's *Sam Spade* on television. Nowhere did he find mention of any special training. It was simply a case, Wilbur concluded, of being in the right place at the right time.

Pushing aside the remains of his breakfast, Wilbur glanced at the Westclock balanced on the windowsill above the kitchen sink. Time to head to the postal station if he didn't want to be late. Following his usual morning routine, he tossed the soiled aluminum breakfast tray into the kitchen garbage, transferred the utensils to the exiles of the kitchen sink, then turned up the volume on his police band radio. Shrugging into his wrinkled, gray raincoat, he pulled his brown Thrift Store fedora low over his eyes and was reaching into the refrigerator, his hand about to close around the tuna fish sandwich he'd put together for today's lunch, when the message crackled into the room.

"There's a problem out at Jensen's Lodge, Inspector," the radio voice sputtered. "Seems they found a dead guy out on one of the hiking trails. Circumstances sound pretty suspicious. I think you might want to get out there right away."

Wilbur hesitated; an idea slyly nudged the edge of his subconscious, then exploded with the impetus of a chute of mail released onto the conveyer belt. *The right place at the right time!* Like a chaotic litter of newborn pups, his thoughts tumbled eagerly over one another. *This just might be the right place, the right time.* With the tip of his thumb, Wilbur tipped the brown fedora to the back of his head and a lopsided grin tilted across his face. From the mirror propped against four tuna fish cans, a cocky likeness of "Mickey Spillane" grinned back at him

*          *          *

In a gesture of frustration, Inspector Branson dragged one hand across the smooth, hairless surface of his forehead, then folded his thick arms across a generous paunch. Unconsciously, he lifted his fingers to tug thoughtfully at his eyebrows. It was a habit infuriating his wife, since he inevitably succeeded in removing the slender hairs, leaving him, so she said, with an uncanny resemblance to a peeled onion with eyes.

Those eyes now probed the early morning fog still hovering above the vacant field. A frown worried his ample brow, then deepened as the Inspector returned his attention to the macabre scene at his feet. Discovered by pre-dawn joggers, the lifeless body of a man lay sprawled in the dew-covered grass, its head twisted into a horrible, unnatural position upon the shoulders.

*Why did this have to happen in my precinct?* Inspector Branson fumed inwardly, ruefully recalling the half-eaten breakfast éclair left sitting on his plate. *Who was this guy, anyway? No identification, no clues to who, or what, had killed him—no footprints, no witnesses, nothing.* Until he had answers to what happened here, Branson knew it was important no word of this grisly assault leak out. The last thing he wanted to deal with was a crowd of hysterical townspeople.

His thoughts interrupted by a disturbance taking place behind him, the Inspector turned in time to see a tall, loose-jointed figure of a man, blatantly ignoring the shouts of his posted guard, duck beneath the yellow, crime-scene tapes cordoning off the area.

"Hey," bellowed Branson. "What to you think you're doing? This is a restricted area!"

A lop-sided grin creased the less-than-handsome face. "'Morning, Inspector." The response, delivered in voice not unlike the grating of sandpaper across rusty metal, suggested a rehearsed braggadocio. "Figured maybe you could use some help."

Inspector Branson could feel the yet-undigested portion of his half-an-éclair threatening to rebel. "Just who in blue blazes are you?" he snapped.

The arrogant smile never leaving his lips, the intruder raised his thumb and tipped a brown fedora to the back of his head. "Peabody's the name," he rasped. "Wilbur Peabody, "private eye," at your service."

"A Private I!" snorted Branson. "Just what I need, a smart ass detective nosing around, stirring up trouble! How'd you find out about this, anyway?"

"Ah, now, Inspector. You wouldn't be asking me to reveal my private sources, would you?" The "private eye's" grin disappeared as he jerked his head toward the body. "What happened to this guy?" Wilbur Peabody,

P.I., stepped closer to peer at the victim. "Gol, looks like his neck is broken," he gasped, turning back to the Inspector. "Got any idea who he is, or was?"

"I haven't finished my investigation, yet," retorted Branson. "Besides, as far as you're concerned, anything I find here is classified information."

Wilbur's gaze moved past the dead man's body. "What's with the dead animals?" He knelt in the damp grass beside the stiffened carcasses then jumped quickly to his feet, eyes wide. "Jeez, their necks are broken, too."

Branson clenched his jaw, cursing inwardly. The caustic retort rising to his lips died there as an eerie, high-pitched wail sliced through the morning stillness. Branson spun toward the sound. Rising in crescendo, it surrounded him, sending chills leap-frogging up his spine. Then, as quickly as it began, it stopped, its echo hanging in the sudden, heavy silence.

"It came from that grove of trees." The quavering voice of the self-appointed private investigator was barely audible, its arrogance suddenly gone.

"Patterson! Mahony!" the Inspector barked. "Go check out the area!"

Faces pale, the blue-uniformed officers glanced uneasily toward one another

"What are you waiting for? Move!"

Two reluctant policemen edged forward, their drawn weapons clutched in white-knuckled fists.

"Do you think that's a good idea?" Wilbur blurted, his voice edged with anxiety. "What if whatever is out there, kills them, too?"

"I don't need you to do my thinking for me," spat the Inspector. Then, "Mahony, Patterson! Stay where you are. Keep an eye on those trees," he ordered as he headed toward the patrol car. "I'm radioing for a back-up."

+          +          +

It was well past noon. The sun, high in the sky, had dissipated all moisture from the tall grass, now trampled and flattened by the passage of many feet. Reinforcements had arrived and were methodically searching the dense grove of evergreens.

"Whoever, or whatever, it was," Branson concluded, "It's gone now. I figure the dead guy, not having any ID on him, was probably just some transient. Anyway, it's over now, Peabody, so there's no sense in you hanging around." With this dismissal, he turned his back on the private investigator and strode to where the crew from the police morgue was bagging the dead body.

Hovering beside his police vehicle, Officers Mahoney and Peterson listened carefully to Inspector Branson's instructions. "Until Detective Hensley sets up surveillance, I want the two of you to stay here and keep an eye on that cedar grove." He lowered his voice. "There's to be no mention to anyone about the boomerang the Search Team found out there. I've got a gut feeling it's connected to this crime and I'm guessing our man will be coming back to retrieve it. When he does, I'm thinking we got our murderer."

*  *  *

Grudgingly, Wilbur Peabody watched the Inspector's retreating figure; witnessed with envy the private conversation being shared with the deputies. A sigh escaped his lips, carrying the last remnant of his earlier air of arrogance with it. His shoulders sagged. He'd so hoped this would turn out to be "the big case" promised aspiring "Private I's" who, according to the magazine ad, could easily enter the exciting world of crime investigation.

Having promptly responded to that ad, along with the required processing fees, Wilbur suffered impatient days of waiting for the slow-in-arriving response. Restless nights were spent reading and re-reading his collection of *Mickey Spillane* novels. He listened hopefully to the police band on his radio each morning as he drove to his "dullsville" job at the post office. Then, this morning, the report of a dead body found out by Jensen's Lodge. He'd been sure this was it, his big chance to break into the exciting world of crime solving; his chance to prove himself as Wilbur Peabody, P.I. But now---Wilbur turned his attention toward the cedar grove. On a case like this, he wondered, what would Mickey Spillane do?

\*          \*          \*

Wilbur moved slowly through the undergrowth, his eyes darting from side to side in search of some hopefully overlooked bit of evidence. A sudden rustling in the bushes startled . . . no . . . frightened him. Quickly, he turned back toward the clearing, but in his haste to flee, his shoe caught on the root of a tree sending him sprawling in a clumsy heap upon the moss-covered earth. He scrambled to his feet in time to see a small gray squirrel scamper up a nearby cedar. Grinning with relief, Wilbur stooped to massage his bruised ankle, then paused as a bit of colored wood, protruding from the greenery, caught his eye.

With the tips of his fingers, he gingerly lifted a crudely carved boomerang from its concealing bed of fern. Carefully wrapping it in his handkerchief, he tucked it into the pocket of his overcoat. One corner of his mouth lifted in a lopsided smile.

"I'm afraid this case isn't over yet, Inspector," he muttered as, with the end of his thumb, he tipped his brown fedora to the back of his head. "No sir, not by a long shot."

\*          \*          \*

Scooping up the scattered letters from below the mail slot, Wilbur dropped them onto the hall table before closing the door of his apartment behind him. He hurried across the room, tugging at the curved bit of wood protruding from his coat pocket where he'd crammed it earlier that morning. Only then did he realize, in jamming the boomerang into the too-small opening, he'd ripped the inside of his pocket, leaving a sizeable hole in the flimsy lining. He'd patch it later, he decided, when he had time to look for the duct tape. But for now, having succeeding in prying that odd shaped piece from its wedged-in location, he laid it upon the kitchen table, next to the *Mickey Spillane* novel he was currently reading.

*So, this is what a real boomerang looks like.* Wilbur studied the crudely carved object. *It looks smaller than the one in National Geographic. Doesn't seem big enough to kill a man.* When he'd stumbled over it, hidden in that clump of fern, he figured it just might be the murder weapon. Now . . . well, now, he wasn't so sure. Running his hand over its smooth surface, he tried to remember anything he might have read about the boomerang. Didn't it return to the thrower? Instinctively, Wilbur snatched his hand back from the object on the table. That would mean the killer could have been in the grove of cedar trees, might even have still been there earlier today, watching the police activity . . . and him. He recalled that eerie keening wail drifting through the morning mist and an involuntary chill shuddered across his shoulders.

Gingerly, he resumed his inspection of the curved missile. *Funny the inspector's men hadn't found it when they searched the woods*, he thought. *Weren't they supposed to be trained for that sort of thing?* The lopsided grin crept across Wilbur's face. Maybe, after all, he did have a special knack for this investigative work.

A glance toward the round Westclock perched on the sill above the sink warned him he was already late for his morning shift at the Post Office. Snatching a carton of milk from inside the refrigerator, he lifted it to his lips, letting the cool liquid slide down his throat. Replacing the half-empty container on its shelf, Wilbur swiped at the white droplets dribbling down his chin and clinging to the sparse hairs of his day-old mustache. Before the refrigerator door swung shut, he grabbed the brown paper sack harboring the tuna fish sandwich he'd prepared the night before.

Struggling back into his overcoat, he paused at the hall table to shuffle through the letters he'd deposited there earlier. For a moment, his job, the boomerang, all were forgotten. Tucked between a postcard advertising a window washing special and a thick packet of money-saver coupons was the letter he'd been waiting for, a letter from the Department of Licensing for Private Investigators. Years of discipline and habit took over. It would have to wait until his lunch hour, Wilbur conceded, slipping the envelope into his coat pocket. The thud as the letter hit the floor reminded Wilbur he'd forgotten to look for the duct tape. Quickly retrieving the errant piece of mail, he tucked it into his shirt pocket. He started out the door, then hesitated, glancing back over his shoulder. A few short steps and he had the boomerang tucked beneath his arm. Several moments later, he was sliding it beneath the front seat of his '56 Chevrolet.

+      +      +

Inspector Branson dragged the palm of his hand across the smoothness of his bald pate. A frown of consternation furrowed its way between his nearly hairless eyebrows. "No activity? None at all?" He pressed the receiver tightly against his ear, listening to the voice of Sargeant Hensley, the surveillance officer he'd posted at Jensen's Lodge. *Maybe I figured this guy wrong.* A moth of uneasiness unfurled its wings inside the Inspector's chest. *If I'm right, if that boomerang is connected to the crime, then the murderer is going to want it back.* He could feel the perspiration gathering on his forehead. *But I thought he'd show by now. I'm sticking my neck way out, gambling with possible evidence.* "Okay, Hensley." He spoke again into the mouthpiece. "Retrieve the boomerang, but careful how you handle it. We'll want to check it for fingerprints."

Dropping the phone into its cradle, the Inspector turned his attention to the memo lying on the desk. *Headquarters was suggesting the victim might have been a guest at the lodge, one who hadn't registered yet.* Unconsciously, the Inspector's fingers plucked at his few remaining hairs of his sparse eyebrows. A sigh escaped his lips. *Might as well check it out. At this point, it's the only lead we've got.*

+ + +

Wilbur's impatience all but consumed him before the big clock on the mailroom wall arrived at the designated noon hour break. With his lunch sack in one hand, and the coveted correspondence clutched in the other, Wilbur scurried to a quiet corner of the lunchroom. Pulling his sandwich from the brown paper bag, he released it from its protective plastic, then wrinkled his nose in disgust. *Tuna fish again! Lordy, how he hated tuna fish. But then, it had been on sale, four cans for a dollar.*

Turning his attention to the letter, Wilbur scanned the first page with its list of requirements for private investigator certification. "A high school education or GED." *Okay, he had that.* "Related employment, which could be a government job, or one providing experience in investigative procedure." *Well, the post office was government, wasn't it? And what about that time he tracked down the lost letter containing the old lady's Social Security check? That should count for something.* He read further. One hundred fifty dollars was the cost of the license, another hundred if he carried a gun. *He'd already saved over a hundred dollars. He could apply for a gun later.*

Wilbur turned to page two listing the duties of a private investigator: observing suspects, conducting surveillance from a car or van, frequently employing the use of binoculars or video cameras. Investigators, he read, are often required to conduct interviews in connection with their cases. Excitement displaced Wilbur's appetite, his offensive tuna sandwich long-since forgotten. He felt sure he already met most of the qualifications. He could pick up a pair of binoculars out of Friday's paycheck. As for the interviewing ... his mind sped back to the boomerang stowed beneath the front seat of his Chevrolet. Who could he interview about the boomerang? He certainly didn't know any Australian aborigines. *But, wait . . . what about that guy who works the second shift, Donavan or Donahue? Isn't he an Aussie? He should know something about aborigine weapons.*

+ + +

It was nearly five-thirty; Wilbur had been waiting in the parking lot since four o'clock. He'd begun to think the second shift worker he waited for might be taking the day off but then he spotted the little yellow Volvo driven by his Australian co-worker. The car had barely come to a halt in its parking space before Wilbur yanked the keys from his own ignition and was hurrying across the parking lot.

"Donavan?" he barked as the tall, sandy haired driver emerged from his vehicle.

Apparently he'd chosen the right name. The man turned. "Yo," came his response.

Quickly closing the distance between them, Wilbur dropped his keys into his coat pocket only to have the resonant clink of metal against concrete remind him of the damaged lining. There was awkward moment while he snatched up the keys, hastily transferred them to the safer confines of his pants pocket then refaced his companion.

"What can I do for you, Mate?" gently prompted the man called Donavan.

Narrowing his eyes, Wilbur raised his hand and, with the end of his thumb, tipped the brown fedora to the back of his head. "Peabody's the name," he countered. "Wilbur Peabody, Private Eye. I'd like to ask you some questions."

The tall, sandy-haired man lifted a skeptical eyebrow. "Say, aren't you the bloke from first shift?"

"That's just my cover," Wilbur growled. "Actually, I'm working on a case. You just might be able to help me."

An amused grin tugged at the corner of the Aussie's mouth. "Fire away, Matie."

A boomerang, Wilbur learned from his informant, is a weapon used by warring Australian aborigines. Usually three feet long, three inches wide, flat on one side, even the smaller version can break the neck of its victim. Due to its curved design, if properly thrown, and if not obstructed by anything larger than a bird or small animal, it will return to its owner.

+ + +

Inspector Branson exploded from his chair, sending it careening across the room on clattering rollers. "What? It's gone?" His white-knuckled fingers gripped the telephone. "The boomerang is gone? How the hell . . .? Get back in here, Hensley," he sputtered into the black mouthpiece. "Be ready to organize a dragnet. You're going to find who took that boomerang and when you do, we just may have our killer."

\* \* \*

Even after Donovan had disappeared through the employee's entrance to the post office, Wilbur made no move to leave the parking lot. Having retrieved it from beneath the front seat, he studied the boomerang he'd taken from the crime scene. Although it wasn't as large as most, according to Donavan, even the smaller model, if thrown with enough force, could kill a man. He tried to remember what Donovan said about the small hole drilled in one end, something about producing a sound to frighten birds earthward so they could be captured in nets. That might explain the keening sound coming from the cedar grove.

Wilbur fingered the small brass pivot attached to the tip of the curved wood in his hand and what appeared to be a bit of fishing line dangling from it. Donavan made no mention of it; probably wasn't that important.

Reluctantly relinquishing the boomerang to the seat beside him, Wilbur turned the key in the ignition and directed his '56 Chevy into the homebound traffic. Pulling to the curb in front of the drab, two-story apartment building with its peeling coat of green paint, Wilbur clambered from the car. He jammed the boomerang into his coat pocket, ignoring the sound of ripping cloth as the already damaged lining obligingly made more room to accommodate the oversized object.

Bounding up the steps, two at a time, eager to give his full attention to the questions ricocheting through his head, Wilbur's steps faltered at the entrance to his second floor apartment. He was sure he'd closed the door this morning, the door now standing slightly ajar. Nudging the scarred paneling with the toe of his shoe, he peered cautiously through the widened opening. The slender hairs of his sparse mustache stirred above his slackened jaw as a sudden gust of surprise escaped Wilbur's lips. The small living space he called home was in shambles. Chairs were overturned, couch cushions sprawled awkwardly upon the cluttered floor, cupboard doors hung open, exposing their meagerly stocked shelves. Drawer contents lay strewn across the counter. A disorderly pile of four-for-a-dollar cans of tuna fish huddled like frightened, homeless children upon the kitchen table.

Wilbur stared in disbelief at the disaster confronting him. Why would anyone break into his apartment, he agonized? He had nothing of value. Stumbling across the room, his legs seemingly turned to rubber, he righted a kitchen chair and sank onto its wooden seat. His overcoat flapped open and the boomerang slipped from his pocket, clattering to the floor. With unseeing eyes, Wilbur stared at the curved weapon lying at his feet. It was a moment before the rocket of reality exploded within his numbed brain. *The boomerang*! Somehow, the killer knew Wilbur had the boomerang . . . the murder weapon . . . and he wanted it back!

His roiling stomach called forth the unpleasant reminder of his partially eaten tuna lunch. Beads of perspiration dampened Wilbur's upper lip, while a choking dryness invaded his throat. *Maybe he should call the police.* In a sudden surge of panic, he was on his feet, snatching the wall phone from its hook. He dialed the numeral nine before he spotted the paperback novel he'd been reading, now lying wedged beneath the corner of the refrigerator. He hesitated. *What would Mickey Spillane do?* Slowly, almost reluctantly, Wilbur dropped the phone back into its cradle.

+ + +

His generous paunch resting against its wooden edge, Inspector Cranston leaned across the reception desk. The guest register belonging to Jensen's Sportsmen's Lodge, attached to its ineffectual yet decorative chain, lay open before him. Across the counter, her blonde hair impeccably coiffured, her long tapered nails brightly lacquered, an attractive young receptionist prudently responded to the Inspector's questions.

"Mr. Henderson's room wasn't ready when he arrived," she offered. "We were short-staffed that day," she went on to explain. "We'd just hosted a large convention group over the weekend." She paused to examine her fingernails for possible imperfections. "Mr. Henderson decided to change into his jogging suit and take some exercise while he waited. He left his bags and street clothes here behind the counter."

Inspector Branson closed the register and slid it across the desk. "Do you know anything about this Mr. Henderson; who he was, why he was here?"

A haughty lift of her chin preceded the young clerk's response. "Sir, we do not divulge personal information regarding our guests."

"This is police business, Miss. I think you'll want to 'divulge'."

Her full, red lips tightened into a petulant pout. " Mr. Henderson is . . . was a land developer," she complied coldly. "He was here to negotiate a purchase of the lodge and our adjoining wild life preserve. I understand Mr. Henderson planned to build a shopping center on the property."

"One more question, Miss. Did anyone else know he was here? Was anyone on duty with you that afternoon?"

She arched her thin, penciled eyebrows. "I suppose Arnold may have known about it. He was the bellhop on duty that day."

"Where can we find this Arnold?"

"He won't be in until later," she lifted her shoulders in a shrug of indifference. "He belongs to some kind of boomerang club. He's usually out practicing when he's not on duty."

The Inspector turned to the two officers at his side. "I think we might want to revisit our crime scene."

+        +        +

Wilbur hunched across the steering wheel, squinting through the round plastic eye- pieces of his new binoculars. Impatiently, he fiddled with the adjustment wheel, but the outline of the cedar trees remained indistinct, fuzzy. The clerk had cautioned him these binoculars were best suited for short-range observation, perhaps even the theatre. But they were on sale and, after all, Wilbur rationalized, binoculars were binoculars. He'd figure out how to use them later. Meanwhile, from what he could tell, there was no activity in the cedar grove. It would be a good time, he decided, to return the boomerang to the fern bed. Then, he could come back, set up surveillance and wait to see who showed up.

Satisfied the coast was clear, he climbed from the car, the boomerang in hand, and made his way to the edge of the cedar grove. The fern bed, its fronds now broken, lay crushed flat against the earth. Wilbur hesitated, glancing about uneasily. *Had he heard something, a squirrel, perhaps? Maybe he should have called the police first.* Tiny cold feet of apprehension crawled up his back. Quickly, he dropped the boomerang into the ravaged clump of fern and turned back toward his car.

It was at that moment Wilbur heard it, the same eerie, keening wail assailing them the first day at the crime scene. Panic urged him to flee, back the way he had come. Fear short-circuited his co-ordination. Wilbur stumbled, fell to his knees, just as something whooshed above his head. He scrambled to his feet, turned to see the whirling object pivoting in mid-air, hurtling back toward him. His pounding heart pumping adrenaline through his body, he lurched to one side. He could feel the tug of a wispy cord wrapping itself around him. As he fought to free himself from the spidery filament, he heard the screech of a car, braking to a stop. Looking up, he saw blue uniformed men spilling from a patrol car, saw a brawny, dark haired young man fleeing toward the shelter of the cedar grove.

"Stop him!" Wilbur screamed. "Stop him! He's the killer!"

Chaotic sounds—running, shouting, distanced themselves from Wilbur as he struggled to free himself from the tangle of thin fishing line imprisoning him. Lying at his feet; still attached to the end of the line by which it could be retrieved; was a boomerang.

+        +        +

A subdued Wilbur stood at the edge of the small crowd gathered on the steps of Jensen's Lodge. Curious onlookers, they watched as the handcuffed prisoner was folded into the back seat of the patrol car; heard his enraged cries, "He was going to destroy everything, the lodge, the wild life. He had to be stopped." They also witnessed the angry glare Inspector Branson flung toward Wilbur before climbing into the patrol car headed to the police station. A scandal-hungry media mingled with the restless knot of observers, collecting its hors d'oeuvres of trivia for the six o'clock news feast.

A voice at his elbow demanded Wilbur's attention. "I understand you were on the scene when the suspect was captured."

Wilbur turned to find the round black knob of a microphone hovering inches from his lips. "Uh, yeah, yeah, I was," his voice scratched across the sandpaper dryness of his throat.

"Is it true, you tried to apprehend the suspect?"

"Well, yeah." Wilbur's voice grew stronger. "Yeah, that's right."

"That was certainly a commendable act of bravery on your part, Mr. . . . Mr. . . . ?"

A lopsided grin slid across Wilbur's face. With the end of his thumb, he tipped the brown fedora to the back of his head. "Peabody," he growled. "Wilbur Peabody, Private Eye."

# TODAY'S FORECAST
# SCATTERED SHOWERS

# THIS, TOO, SHALL PASS

Red and green lights burned brightly among green boughs.

Softly falling snow muted the insolent sounds of traffic.

Impatient children awaited their jolly red-suited benefactor.

And the watch went on cutting time with its little saw.


The knotted fist of tension beat rhythmically behind closed eyes.

The condemned man huddled in the corner of his darkened cell.

Choices recalled, he yearned for a chance to relive his life.

And the watch went on cutting time with its little saw.


Her heart overflowed with the wonder of her love.

Nervous fingers searched for disobedient strands of hair.

Anxiously, the woman anticipated the arrival of her beloved.

And the watch went on cutting time with its little saw.


The joyous sound of laughing children.

The quiet sobs of a man's lost hope.

The soft murmurs of a woman's love.

And the watch went on cutting time with its little saw

# JUST ONE MORE HOUR

He'd forgotten how good it felt, warm sand caressing the soles of his feet, squishing between bare toes. Shoes, tied together by their laces, dangling loosely about his neck, pant legs rolled halfway up his shins, Jerry strode along the ocean's edge. He made no effort to avoid the tide's occasional surge of water swirling about his ankles, washing away the clinging gritty granules. The first timid light of dawn gave way to the boldness of the rising sun, silhouetting the fleet of tiny fishing boats bobbing about on the undulating horizon. Gulls, wings spread wide, drifted lazily on the wind's current.

There was something soothing, almost hypnotic about the constant movement of the ocean, Jerry decided, even therapeutic. He had come here this morning, hoping to find answers to the tangled mess of his life. Now, he found himself wishing for more than the empty solace these placid ocean waters could offer. He needed someone to talk to; someone who would understand what he was going through. Unexpectedly, the image of his father invaded his thoughts. Yes, the old man would understand, Jerry admitted. But, even if they'd been on speaking terms, now it was too late. His father was gone forever, the rift between them unresolved.

"Damn," Jerry hissed, startling the sandpipers skittering along the beach in front of him. He shook his head, hoping to dislodge the guilt, the regret, always accompanying memories of his father. Reluctantly, he let his mind replay those earlier months of anger and pain. *Selfish, egocentric*, Jerry called his father when he learned of the divorce plans. Jerry and his kid sister were grown by then, no longer needing their father's financial support. Still, Jerry had condemned his father for what he considered abandonment of marriage vows, disruption of the family; condemned him, Jerry conceded, for the very thing he was about to do.

Defensive, he reviewed justification for his own proposed actions. For a long time now, he'd felt smothered in this little hick town, trapped by his going-nowhere sales job at the cycle shop. Then, just last week, out of the blue, he'd been offered his own dealership in Atlanta. Suddenly, the world opened up before him. He couldn't wait to share the news with his wife. Jerry kicked at a tiny sand crab scurrying across his path. His clay-footed wife refused to consider the move.

"This is my home," Donna argued. "I grew up in Rockford. My family is here. This house we live in, our home, has been in my family over a hundred years. I can't believe you'd ask me to leave it."

It wasn't until then Jerry realized how much they'd grown apart. Donna fit into the small town community, content with a social life of quilting bees, gossiping over afternoon tea with the rest of these dull, small-minded housewives. He wanted to savor life, share its adventures— conquer its challenges.

Jerry sidestepped an empty clamshell discarded by a foraging seagull. He couldn't stay here, he agonized, watching his life just ebb away with the years. If Donna wouldn't go with him, he would go alone. His kids would just have to understand.

He hesitated, mid-stride, forcing himself to inspect the unwelcome thoughts intruding upon his miseries. Had his father felt this way? Had his mother been like Donna? He tried to remember his mother ever accompanying his councilman father on any of his business trips, joining him at any promotional social functions. Jerry could recall only the pleasant, slightly plump woman who made sure he and his sister had clean clothes, baked goodies and an endless flow of mealtime delights. She'd been a good mother . . . but had she been a good wife?

Jerry knew a sudden overwhelming sorrow, regret for having waited too long to mend the distance between them, to tell his father, too late, he finally understood.

Staring, unseeing, at the ground before him, Jerry's his eyes suddenly focused upon a bright object protruding from the sand at his feet. Stooping he pulled it from its gritty prison, sending a now homeless sand crab sidestepping to safety. Jerry brushed his sleeve across the object, which appeared to be a lamp of some sort. His commiseration momentarily diverted by childhood memories of the "Arabian Nights" and "Aladdin" with that wonderful lamp, Jerry grinned.

"Hey," he chuckled to himself. "Maybe there's a genie inside who'll me grant all my wishes." Playfully, he rubbed his hand across the tarnished surface. "Let's see, I wish . . . I wish . . . . The smile disappeared from Jerry's lips, the merriment from his eyes. "I wish," he whispered softly, "I wish I could spend one day, even just one more hour, with my father, talk to him, let him know . . . .."

A nervous laugh tore itself from Jerry's lips. *What was he doing, acting like a goofy ten-year-old?* With a shrug of indifference, he carelessly tossed the brass lantern back onto the sand where eager fingers of salty water rushed forward to reclaim their treasure. Hands jammed into his pockets, Jerry resumed his walk on the beach. "Ya dumb dork," he muttered. The raucous scolding from a gray gull, swooping overhead was less forgiving.

Jerry's legs were beginning to tire . . . the muscles of his calves feeling the unaccustomed strain of walking on sand. He glanced ahead to where a boardwalk fronted a row of convenience shops. Turning from the water's edge, he crossed the beach to a bench at the end of the boardwalk and sank gratefully onto its slatted surface. Brushing the sand from between his toes, he shoved them into the socks he retrieved from him pocket, then slipped his feet into his shoes. He glanced at his watch. Ten o'clock; he still had time to kill. The appointment with his attorney wasn't until eleven. He returned his gaze to where, on the sparkling sunlit waters, a congregation of screeching seagulls noisily discussed the day's itinerary.

Lost in thought, Jerry didn't hear the woman approach.

"Excuse me, is this seat vacant?" A middle-aged woman hovered over the bench; beside her an old man leaned unsteadily upon his cane. "Are you expecting someone or is it okay if my father rests here for awhile?"

"Oh, no, no." Jerry slid along the bench to make room. "I mean no, I'm not expecting anyone. Please, sit down, sit down."

With a heavy sigh, the old man lowered himself onto the bench.

"Be back in a bit, Daddy." The woman patted the man's shoulder. "Enjoy the sun."

The old man grunted his response as the woman turned and hurried back the way they had come.

They sat in silence, the old man and Jerry, staring out across the water where a slight breeze now teased tiny whitecaps onto the once flat surface.

"Nice day." The old man's voice was soft with age.

"Yes, yes, it is," Jerry agreed.

Another moment of silence and then, "Sun feels good."

"Yes, yes, it does, doesn't it?"

"Ellie used to like coming down here to the beach." It was a moment before the old gentleman spoke again. "But, she's gone, now."

"Oh, I'm sorry," Jerry acknowledged politely.

"We'd be married sixty-five years tomorrow." Then, before Jerry could respond, "You married?"

"Well, yes, I am," Jerry stammered, remembering his appointment. "Sort of."

A few moments of uneasy silence followed.

"You not working today?"

*Had the old man no sense of propriety?* "I have an appointment. I took the day off."

"Ah, I see." The old man nodded, tapping his cane on the edge of the boardwalk.

For some reason, Jerry felt the need to vindicate himself. "I . . . I'm a salesman at the Rockford Cycle Shop. They're not too busy Tuesdays."

"You like the job?"

"It's okay, I guess." His next words sprang unexpectedly from Jerry's lips. "They've offered me my own dealership in Atlanta."

"Lot more goin' on up there in the big city," the old man conceded. "Be mighty hard to turn down an offer like that. You gonna take it?"

"I . . . I don't know yet."

"Hmmm. Wife doesn't want to move?"

"Her people are 'Old Rockford'," Jerry started to explain, then stopped.

The old man interrupted the awkward silence that followed. "Life's not meant to be an easy road," he began, staring off toward the open water of the ocean. "Full of hills and valleys. I always looked at it like a whole series of plateaus, a ladder leadin' up to each one.' His trembling hand slashed a wavering row of imaginary lines in the air. "Now, you can just stay in the valleys where it's nice and comfortable, but if you want to know what's waiting on that plateau, you gotta climb the ladder. Trouble is, when you get to the top there's always another ladder, waiting to take you still higher. You gotta decide where you wanna' be, how far you wanna' climb. If you've got someone willing to climb them ladders alongside you, that's good." The old man paused, some past memory glazing his eyes. "Two folks don't always grow the same, even when they're man and wife." The old man's voice grew softer. "Ellie and me lived on the farm when we first married. She liked the farm, but me, I wanted something better. Ellie didn't want to climb no ladder but she did it, 'cause she knew it was what I wanted.

"We came to Rockford, I got me a good factory job. Things were fine for awhile, but then I got a chance for a better paying job, off in Minneapolis."

Jerry shifted uneasily on the bench. *Why is he telling me this? Maybe I should just go, leave the old man to his memories.* But before Jerry could excuse himself, the tired voice continued.

"If I'd taken the job, I wouldn't have to be living with my daughter, now that Ellie's gone; my daughter wouldn't have to be going back to work to pay my medical bills. But Ellie didn't want to climb another ladder." A sigh escaped the old gentleman's lips. "She gave in to me once. I figured this time, we should do what she wanted." Silence hung between the two men again with only the sound of the old man's cane, tapping against the boardwalk. "I'm too old for climbing now, but I guess I'll always wonder what was at the top to that other ladder."

"We have to go now, Daddy." The middle-aged woman was back. "It's time for your medication and then I have to get to work."

Gripping the worn handle of his cane, the old man rose laboriously, his aged joints loudly protesting. He rested for a moment on his cane, then turned back, his eyes meeting those of his younger companion. Jerry's heart stumbled, his breath hovered, forgotten somewhere in his chest as he found himself staring into a pair of clear blue eyes, recognized the familiar spark he'd known in another pair of eyes, belonging to his past.

"A man's gotta do what a man's gotta do." The old man's voice was scarcely audible. "He only hopes his kids will understand."

Tears crowded into Jerry's eyes. "I do," he heard himself whisper. "I do understand."

Wrinkled cheeks folded to accommodate the old man's gentle smile. He tilted his head in a barely perceptible nod.

Misty-eyed, Jerry watched as the old man, leaning heavily upon his daughter's arm, moved slowly down the boardwalk. Jerry glanced at his watch. It was eleven fifteen. Somehow, the missed appointment with his lawyer didn't matter . . . he suddenly realized he wasn't ready to make a decision yet. He glanced anxiously down the boardwalk, hoping for another glimpse of the old man. But he was gone, lost among the late morning crowd filling the beachfront.

For one, almost irrepressible, moment, Jerry wanted to dash back down the beach, back to where he'd left the lantern. But he knew he'd not find it there. The restless ocean would have carried it away to toss upon some other sandy beach where, perhaps even now, another troubled soul was wishing for just one more hour.

# AID CALL

Traffic was light on a Tuesday, late afternoon, so it took us less than ten minutes to cover the distance between the station and the quiet suburban street on the outskirts of town. Still, several members of the police force, apparently dispatched ahead of us, were already taking apart the front door of the little gray stucco house.

My partner, Ed, and I were responding to a 911 call from an anxious neighbor, concerned when it had been over a week since she'd seen the man who lived in the house next to hers. Apparently, she also called the police. A battered old Chevy sat in the driveway; unclaimed newspapers accumulated on the front porch. A forlornly neglected mailbox tilted crazily from the one bolt precariously securing it to the side of the building. No one, the uniformed officer informed us, was responding to the persistent summons of the doorbell.

The door now removed from its hinges, we stepped across the thresh hold and into the dim interior of a small living room. An Indian motif blanket, silhouetted eagles winging across its dingy brown and white surface, covered the doorway to the kitchen while another faded blanket of the same design, but different color, obscured the access to a hallway leading, presumably, to the bedrooms. Weathered bamboo shades hung askew across the room's picture window, discouraging any hint of light that might seek entry into the darkened, unheated room

Like undisciplined children, assorted items of soiled wardrobe sprawled insolently across the room's two overstuffed chairs. A pair of well-worn western boots, resembling a duo of luckless gunfighters, lay mercilessly abandoned where they had fallen. Equally unfortunate victims, broken-back Nikes rested beside them in ugly repose, ragged tongues unrestrained by laces hanging loosely from their gaping mouths.

A soggy, half-eaten slice of pizza saturated the scattered pile of unopened mail obliterating the top of a coffee table. Discarded peanut shells crunched underfoot, grinding themselves into the soiled, abused carpet as we crossed to the rumpled bunching of blankets trembling upon the couch.

Cautiously, Ed lifted the edge of a tattered quilt, pulling it back to reveal a pair of frightened, red-rimmed eyes peering from a pale, bearded face. The stench of an unwashed body and sour vomit rose to intercept us. Despite the fact the man was swathed in several layers of clothing, he shivered uncontrollably. With claw-like fingers, he snatched the quilt from Ed's hand, clutched it protectively beneath his chin. I felt the familiar knot forming in my stomach.

"It's okay, man." Ed knelt beside the couch, his voice soft, reassuring. It never ceased to amaze me how Ed's voice could always soothe, both the frightened victim and the violent perpetrator. "We're here to help you, guy. Your neighbor was worried about you."

While the warm honey of Ed's voice flowed through the room, I mentally assessed the papers littering the table before us. A soiled, tattered envelope caught my eye. Carefully, I lifted it from its nest of debris. There was no writing on the outside so I lifted the flap to examine the contents. The envelope was empty except for a dusting of white powder-like substance cowering in one bottom corner. Closing the flap, I tucked the evidence into the pocket of my jacket. When we got back to the station, I would turn it over to the Lab for analysis, but I was already fairly certain of what they would find.

By now, Ed had raised our subject to a sitting position. Huddled on the edge of the couch, the man hunched over his lap, silently picking at some unseen annoyance on the back of his hand.

"We're going to take you down to the station, buddy. We're going to get you the help you need," Ed explained patiently, his face inches from that of the sick man. "When was the last time you ate, fella?" Ed prompted.

The man's brow furrowed then his eyes glittered with an unnatural brightness. "Today," he announced proudly. "Lunch," the bearded chin shot out defiantly. "I had lunch today with an Indian chief."

Ed rose to his feet and placed a hand beneath the man's armpit, indicating with a nod that I was to do the same on his other side. For an instant, our glances met above the matted, unwashed head of the addict and I saw mirrored in Ed's eyes, the same question I'm sure he saw in mine.

*Why? In God's name, why?*

# STORM WATCH

From the seeming safety of the dock, I peered expectantly across the choppy waters of a restless bay. Fifty-mile-an-hour winds, the weatherman predicted—definitely a storm of some consequence, promising a spectacular show as only Mother Nature can offer. I'd chosen my grandstand seat on the marina's dock as the perfect viewing point.

Overhead, a leaden sky hung like a cold, wet shroud. Hovering above me, a seagull of a dingy slightly lesser, gray, engaged in a "Mexican standoff" with the capricious air currents. Visible in the distance, just off Point Robertson, a glistening wall of frozen rain connected sky with water as the approaching storm advanced menacingly down the channel. Driven before the fury of the wind, white crested waves leaped into the air, snapping angrily at the icy pellets peppering the surf.

Engrossed in the unfolding drama between battling elements, I failed to notice how quickly the squall was sweeping northward until, with alarming suddenness, the storm was swirling about me, the illusion of the dock's comparative safety, shattered. Belligerent gusts of wind flung hands-full of stinging hail into my face, tore insolently at my clothing, invaded the protective cocoon of my parka, boldly snatching it from my head.

For a moment, I closed my eyes against the relentless onslaught, opening them in time to see, too late, the gigantic wall of water towering above me. It hovered for a moment like some hungry predator; then flung itself onto the dock, engulfing me in its frigid, salty arms. Ripping the air from my lungs before moving on, it crashed against the brick wall of the building housing the restrooms, splashing its way across the concrete until it became no more than a harmless rippling pool covering the parking lot.

Clutching my now drenched jacket about me, I quickly sought refuge behind the protective, waist-high railing lining the boardwalk. Turning back toward the sea, I squinted into the roiling turbulence consuming the bay. Excitement warmed the blood rushing through my veins, discouraging the chilling dampness that would embrace me.

Then I saw it, barely visible, just off Point Robertson, tumbling and tossing about like a bit of rudderless cork, a sailboat, riding the crest of the raging waters. But, just as suddenly as it appeared, it was gone. Salt stung my tongue as I licked lips suddenly gone dry. Anxiously, my eyes raked the horizon. Had I imagined it? Surely my eyes were playing tricks upon me. Only a crazy man would set sail in a storm of this magnitude. Of course, there was always the possibility the skipper had been caught unawares, but that seemed highly unlikely. Wind warnings had been broadcast easily a full, twenty-four hours preceding the storm.

The breath trapped in the back of my throat spewed from my salt-encrusted lips as, once again, the little craft appeared. Held high, like a touch-down football, it teetered for a moment atop a leaping wave, its red and white sails flapping helplessly, and then it was gone again.

I'm not certain how long I stood there, watching in spellbound horror, as the small craft waged its choreographed battle with the violent sea—riding the crest of a wave one moment, wallowing in a watery trough the next. Then, an unsettling thought stirred the hairs at the base of my neck. What if the skipper is unable to radio for help, or is an untrained novice, an amateur, caught in this terrible storm? Even to me, as little as I knew about sailing, it was obvious the sails should have been lowered. Yet, seemingly no attempt was being made to secure the boat's three sails, two red and one smaller white one, billowing in the merciless winds.

I peered intently across the agitated waters. There was no sign of the small craft. It should have resurfaced by now. Had it capsized? Was the desperate crew, even now, clinging helplessly to their overturned boat? Anxiously, I glanced about the now deserted marina. Everyone seemed to have sought shelter from the storm's brutality. Only one other shared the boardwalk, an older man, who, caught by the same wave that attacked me, had also moved to the protection of the rail-enclosed area.

His hands were jammed into the pockets of a navy blue peacoat, its upturned collar all but obliterating the gray tufts of hair peeking from beneath his billed fisherman's cap. Hunching into the wind, he gazed stoically across the water, apparently oblivious to the tragedy I'd just witnessed. He glanced in my direction as I approached him, then away; his indifference I had not the patience to deal with at the moment.

Frantically scanning the emptiness of the parking lot, I spotted the glow of light illuminating the harbormaster's office. Ignoring the arctic water slopping over my shoe tops, I splashed across the inundated concrete. Bursting through the doorway, I flung myself, breathless, across the counter. Surprise etched the startled faces of two men sharing the duty as they contemplated the wild-eyed, water-soaked, salt-encrusted apparition confronting them.

"A boat!" I panted. "A sailboat! Capsized off the Point!"

"Calm down, Ma'am." The older man moved toward the counter. "Calm down. What is this about a sailboat?"

"Off the point!" My voice rose an octave. ""They need help! I was watching them when they just disappeared!"

The younger man joined his companion. "That's odd," he interrupted. "No craft has left the marina today. We've had no calls from anyone in distress."

A grenade of irritation exploded inside my chest, shattering my self-control. I made no effort to staunch the sarcasm dripping from my words. "I am not an hysterical old woman!" I snapped. "I did not imagine it! I saw the boat! Are you going to do something or should I find help elsewhere?"

"All right, lady. All right." An edge crept into the officer's voice. "Suppose you tell us what you saw. A sailboat, you say. Would you describe it for us?"

"Of course," I agreed, only slightly placated. "It had three sails, two red and one white. I couldn't see the boat clearly, but I could see the sails. They were . . . "

The two men exchanged uneasy glances. The younger man turned back to his desk. The older officer cleared his throat "Ma'am," he began. I felt myself bristle at his condescending tone. "Sometimes, especially in a storm, our eyes can play tricks on us." I felt my face flush with anger. Averting his eyes, the officer paused, then cleared his throat again. "The call may have gone to another station. "We'll check it out ma'am."

Inwardly writhing with frustration, I whirled from the counter and stomped from the office, the resounding slam of the door leaving no doubt as to the depth of my irritation. Determined to carry my cause to a higher authority, I headed toward my car.

"Ma'am?"

The commanding tone of a gruff voice halted me, mid-stride. I turned to find myself facing the old man from the pier.

"Don't be upset with them fellas in there," he offered. "There ain't nothin' they can do. They get reports like this every time they's a bad storm; sailboat running full sail, two red, one white. They ain't never found a trace of the boat."

"Then, you saw it, too?" I interrupted excitedly.

The old man's head bobbed up and down. "Yup, lots of times. Always when they's a bad storm, like this one."

"But . . . what . . .?" Confusion had displaced my anger.

The old fisherman paused as he studied the leaden skies. "It was back in the early forties," he began to explain to some unseen entity over my left shoulder. "This fella moved into town and right off, got hisself a sailboat, a right trim little ketch. Outfitted it with all that red canvas, just left the jib white. A mite fancy for these parts in them days. Folks said he made a livin' writin' stuff." He paused, his gray brows courting

one another above the narrow bridge of his nose. "Poetry, I think it was."
He shook his head. "He was a strange one, that one."

Anyways," my self-appointed informant went on. "He set up
housekeepin' on that boat, took it out most every day over to the Point.
Dang good sailor he was, too, knew how to handle a boat. 'Twarn't no
doubt he knowed enough to reef the mainsail and hoist the storm jib
in a high wind. That's why folks could never figure why he set sail one
day, in full riggin', right into a bugger of a storm."

The aged mariner pushed the cap off his forehead and his pale
watery eyes met mine. "That was the last anyone seen of him, or his
boat . . . 'cept, when they's a big storm, like today. Then, them red sails
show up off the Point." He chuckled, jerking his head toward the marina
office. "Pretty near drives them fellas crazy."

Shrugging his shoulders as if to dismiss the incredibility of his story,
the old man raised his fingers to the visor of his cap. A half-smile lifted
the corner of his mouth. "Well, anyways, you have yourself a good day,
Ma'am."

I could only stare speechlessly after his retreating figure as, coat
collar turned up, hands closeted in his pockets, the old man returned
to his storm watch at the end of the pier.

# NIGHTWATCH

The daylight hours are shrinking, drawn into darkness by the approach of the winter solstice. Once the warm rays of the late afternoon sun lingered lazily in my garden, lovingly caressing bright, fragrant blossoms before reluctantly slipping into the gentle softness of dusk.

But now, in late October, it is a different sun that, as if eager to be elsewhere, drops with a suddenness behind the trees, leaving the last remnants of daylight to be greedily snatched away by the clutching fingers of darkness.

On soundless, velvet-shod feet, furtive shadows of night slip from behind my rhododendron, creep stealthily from beneath the hydrangea, crowding into my garden. In ever-increasing numbers, they surround my house, pressing against my windows, halted only by the courageous circle of artificial light illuminating my entryway. Restlessly, they reconnoiter, lurking at the outer edges of my pale fortress.

Through the long hours, they skulk and dart about my yard, holding my small piece of Eden captive, until, at last, the tardy light of dawn gradually disperses their army, sending them slinking into unseen corners. Yet, even as the weakened sun struggles across the winter sky, they crouch, impatiently, in their secret hiding places . . . waiting for the night.

# CROSSROADS

Crouching behind a sheltering prymadallis hedge, I peered cautiously down the quiet deserted street, then toward the vague outline of a brick rambler huddled at the end of the driveway. A cold, pitiless moon glared through the stark limbs of a denuded maple tree—the moon of thieves and crossroads, its pale watery light etching ghostly shadows, creating a strangely hostile landscape. Sharp, merciless shrubbery clutched at the thin nylon of my black windbreaker, cruelly stabbing the tender skin beneath as, like a thief in the night, I cowered among its branches.

The sudden realization of the awful price I'd pay, if caught, dropped across my shoulders like a cold, heavy mantle. Fear forced a surge of bile into the back of my throat. *What was I doing here?* I thought I'd left this life behind, chosen a different path than the one Rick traveled. Why did he choose to call *me* tonight? I felt the anger knotting in my chest, twisting my insides. Then, just as quickly as it had come, it disappeared, displaced by a shameful sense of disloyalty. I owed Rick my life. He was the best friend I'd ever had, even if he was a drug dealer.

The eerie stillness of the night was shattered as, several blocks away, a restless dog, responding to its primal instincts, sent its plaintive lament into the moonlit sky. Its cry stirred childhood memories of tales of a full moon and the bloom of the wolfbane. A shiver crawled up my spine and into my scalp. Once, it would have sent me scurrying to the safety of my bed. Tonight, I can but pull the collar of my jacket more closely about my throat.

I glanced apprehensively toward the shadow-shrouded building at the end of the lane. There was no movement, no sign of life. Rick said to wait. And so, I wait. My thoughts scurry about like a nervous crab, scurrying toward darkened corners where I've chosen to tuck away my unpleasant past. With little urging, memories slink from exile. I was pretty strung out on drugs, crawling about in my slimy pit of existence when I met Rick; no money, no place to stay; couldn't remember when I'd last eaten. Then, on the street, I heard about this fellow who ran a marijuana operation out of his garage, how sometimes, during harvesting, he'd let you work off the price of a fix. I was desperate, a real basket case. I don't know why Rick took me in. Because he was, basically, a good guy, I guess.

Rick didn't do drugs himself. He had a wife and a kid. As for dealing marijuana, "They're gonna buy it from somebody," he rationalized. "It might as well be me." For whatever reason, he chose to pull me out of the gutter. For a fact, I know I'd be dead now if he hadn't. Somehow, he got me back on the right track, got me a job as security guard, a nice apartment across town. I'd been "clean" for over a year now, was beginning to feel good about myself—until tonight, when I got the phone call from Rick.

"I need your help, man. You're the only one I can trust." His voice had been tight with urgency. "They're planning on taking me down tomorrow."

I squinted nervously down the darkened driveway. Where was Rick? Had something gone wrong? My eyes smarted with the effort to distinguish some sign of life. A shadow detached itself from the large honeysuckle bush swallowing the front porch. I stepped from my hiding place.

"Rick?" I whispered into the darkness.

At the end of the block, a car turned the corner, its headlamps splashing an unwelcome path of light onto the street. The moon's ethereal sculptures scurried for cover while the brittle arms of the hedge greedily welcomed me back into its brambly bosom. The car edged slowly along the pavement, pausing long enough at the end of the driveway for me to make out the lettering across its side, "City Police."

I waited until the car disappeared at the far end of the street before I disengaged myself from the possessive clutches of my prickly sanctuary.

"Steve!" I heard my name hissed into the night air. "Over here! Hurry!"

I sprinted to where I'd last seen the vague shadow of a man. A hand clutched my arm, dragging me through the doorway of a darkened garage. A dim light flicked on, reflecting from foil-lined walls, distorting the face of my friend.

"Thanks for coming, man." Rick's words crowded from his mouth like frightened sheep. "We gotta work fast. Word's out on the street the cops are onto my setup. They're planning to take me down tomorrow. We gotta get rid of this stuff tonight."

The wavering beam of Rick's flashlight illuminated the pickup truck parked inside the garage. Growing-lights, already dismantled, were stored inside its canopy. I began ripping foil from the walls, while Rick flung buckets and pots filled with new and full-grown plants alike, on top of the electrical equipment. The earlier chill of the night was forgotten as perspiration soaked my suddenly too-warm clothing. We paused, only once, at the sound of a car cruising by on the street outside. Two hours later the deed was done; all paraphernalia tightly packed into the back of the pickup.

"One more favor, man." Rick's face glistened with sweat, the muscles of his jaw, tight. "I hate to ask this." He hesitated; then, "I've sent the wife and kid over to her mother's. That's where I'm headed now." He closed his eyes for a moment; his face contorting with his struggle for words. "You know I can't park the truck there. They've got me under surveillance. There's the wife . . . my kid."

I watched as Rick drew a deep breath into his lungs, watched as he let it slowly escape from his lips. I knew what he was going to say. I knew I didn't want to hear it.

"Just for tonight, buddy. No one will notice it in that big parking lot outside your building. I promise it will be gone by morning. I just need time."

Sometimes there is only one right thing to do, even when you know it's the wrong thing. I dropped Rick off at his in-laws, then drove the truck, laden with its illegal cargo, back across town where I angle-parked it in a space at the far edge of the apartment parking lot. Tossing the keys into the glove compartment, I hurried across the blacktop and ducked into the building's side entrance.

I didn't sleep much that night. As if by a magnet, I was drawn to my second floor window overlooking the parking lot. I'd parked the truck as far from a street light as possible, yet it seemed to have an inner glow of its own; a vengeful informer, eager to reveal its passive involvement in this felony. I cowered behind my curtain, alert to every little sound, expecting the knock on the door that would fill my room with cops.

Exhausted, I finally dozed off about four a.m., only to be awakened by the alarm I'd set for seven. Groggily, I struggled into my work uniform, trying to ignore the early morning light peeking through my window, knowing it also illuminated the parking lot— and the truck. Nerves were churning my empty stomach into a state of nausea. Finally, I could no longer suppress the urge. Reluctantly, I drew back the curtain, let my gaze crawl across the parking lot. For a moment, I forgot to breathe. The space where I'd left the pickup was empty. The truck was gone!

For the next few days, I searched the newspapers for any report of a local drug bust. There was none. I didn't dare call Rick's house, and I didn't know his in-law's number. For some reason, I felt relieved about that, as if it excused me for not following up. It also made me feel guilty for being too much of a coward to stand by a friend who once stood by me. I *had* been there for him, given him all the help I could. But had it been enough?

# THE WOMAN NEXT DOOR

I don't know exactly what time it was. I hadn't bothered to check the clock on my nightstand when I struggled out of bed. But, I was sure it was well past midnight. The Mongolian beef I had for dinner came back to haunt me and I awoke feeling as if I had a mouth full of cotton. I stumbled down stairs and flicked on the light above the kitchen sink. Filling a glass with water, I lifted it to my lips and let the cool, soothing liquid slide down my parched throat.

As I lowered the glass, I glanced out the window and was mildly surprised to notice my neighbor's light was also on. We lived on a cul de sac where the houses were situated so my kitchen faced my neighbor's living room. In spite of the close proximity of dwellings, I scarcely knew the woman living next door other than by the name stenciled on her curbside mailbox— *Miriam Anderson*— and that, maybe fifty years old, she lived alone.

An attractive older gentleman had helped her move in about six months ago, hanging pictures, arranging the heavier furniture. They seemed compatible, but though he visited her frequently during daytime hours, his car was never parked in her driveway overnight. Whatever their relationship, it seemed all Miriam needed. She kept pretty much to herself and, while she politely returned my greetings, it was obvious my new neighbor had no interest in nurturing a friendship.

I turned on the kitchen faucet to refill my glass when a movement across the way caught my eye. Miriam had entered her living room and begun removing pictures from the wall. I quickly switched off the overhead light and stepped back from the window. I didn't want her to catch me observing her. I knew I should return to my bed, but my curiosity held me captive.

Miriam's slender figure flitted about the room like a woman obsessed, a humming bird in human form, wings moving too fast to be seen without a stop-motion camera. As I watched, she totally stripped the walls of decoration, then quickly re-hung the pictures, but in different locations. Then, to my amazement, she began moving the furniture. In less than half an hour, the entire room was re-arranged. Arms akimbo, in what seemed an almost defiant stance, she stood back, surveying her work. Then, switching off the light, she left the room.

I had little choice but to return to my bed where my insatiable curiosity kept me tossing fitfully for the next hour. I wondered why, scarcely five feet tall and surely weighing little more than a hundred pounds, this petite little lady would tackle such arduous labor at this hour; why she hadn't waited for her gentleman friend to help her. There, in the darkness of my room, it suddenly occurred to me; I hadn't seen the gentleman around for over a week.

At approximately the same time the following night, my inner alarm roused me, no doubt set off by my wanton curiosity. I crept cautiously down the stairwell to my kitchen window. Once again, the light was on in Miriam's living room. Once again, she was darting about the room with the same possessed intensity; removing pictures from the wall, tugging at the heavy furniture. I shivered, partly in anticipation; partly because I'd forgotten my slippers and my feet were cold. Still, I could not leave my snooper's post.

As on the night before, Miriam completed her re-arranging in just under half an hour. Only this time, everything was back exactly as she and her friend first arranged it. Her shoulders seemed to sag as, tucking an errant strand of graying hair behind her ear, she once again viewed her handiwork. Moving slowly now, my tiny neighbor paused in the doorway, glancing wistfully about the room before turning off the light. A gentle rain had begun to fall, sending rivulets of water trickling, like tears, down my window. Returning to my bed, a strange uneasiness kept me awake until the wee hours.

I was beginning to feel like Jimmy Stewart as, for the third night, I stood in my darkened kitchen, peering out my own *Rear Window*. I took small solace from the fact at least I was not using binoculars. Miriam's light was on, and, as before, she lifted the wall hangings from their hooks. But tonight was different. Miriam's movements were those of an old woman, and instead of repositioning pictures, she stacked them in a neat pile beside the door. She gripped the arm of the couch, as if to move it, but, instead, crumpled onto its cushions. Like a wadded bit of newspaper, she huddled in that fetal position, feet tucked beneath her, face in her hands. She was crying.

I wanted to go to her, offer her comfort. But then, I would have to confess I'd been spying on her. I crept back upstairs and, wrapped in guilt, crawled back into my bed where I spent the remainder of the night, grappling with the merciless nagging of a tormented conscience.

The sky was beginning to lighten in the East before I finally dozed off. I couldn't have slept for more than a few minutes when I was awakened by a tumultuous racket. Voices were shouting, lights were flashing; someone was pounding on a door. Peeking from behind my bedroom curtains, I discovered a yellow aid truck blocking my driveway. Clustered on the porch next door, several firemen were attempting to gain entry to Miriam's house. By the time I located my robe and slippers and dashed downstairs, four firemen were emerging from her house carrying a stretcher bearing Miriam's frighteningly still form. I clutched the sleeve of a fifth fireman as he stepped from the porch.

"What happened?" I begged. "What's wrong?"

Turning toward me, his captain's badge reflecting the flashing red of the emergency light, he tugged a notebook and pencil from his pocket. "You know the woman who lives here?" he demanded.

"Miriam," I responded dutifully. "Miriam Anderson. What's happened?"

"What about relatives? Is there someone we can call?"

I immediately thought of Miriam's gentleman friend, then realized I didn't know his name, or where he lived. "I . . . I don't know her that well," I stammered. "What happened?" I persisted. "Is she okay?"

The captain paused a moment, deciding, I supposed, whether he should share the information with me. "Attempted suicide." His reply was sharp, angry. "Took some pills then changed her mind. Happens a lot. Sometimes," he snapped his notebook shut. "Sometimes, they wait too long before they call us."

Siren screeching, the aid car sped out onto the street. A chill crowded about my heart as I stood watching until the yellow blur disappeared around the corner, listening until its siren was no more than a faint wail in the distance.

"I'm sorry," I whispered into the pre-dawn half-light. "Forgive me."

A capricious November wind snatched at a pile of dry leaves, twirling them in a wild pirouette along the deserted sidewalk before dropping them at my feet, then whirling off in search of new partners. Shivering, I pulled my robe tightly about me and turned back to my house and the comfort of my still-warm bed. But, I knew an unforgiving conscience lay there awaiting me. It would be a long while before I would again know the undisturbed peace of a full night's sleep.

# TODAY'S FORECAST
# BLUSTERY AND COLD

# LOST MOMENT

It was there . . . so close . . . like a crystal prism, sparkling in the sunlight. All I had to do was reach out, touch it, and it would be mine . . . Happiness.

I hesitated, only a moment, but a moment too long. Then, it was gone, the promise of ecstasy.

The door closed on that glimpse of heaven and I was facing the prospect of pain and desolation, stretching before me like a long winding road to hell.

I was plunged into despair, a deep, dark, all-consuming despair, draining the very life from my soul, leaving only a black, gaping emptiness that begged for the obliterating solace of death.

I cry out to what I had believed to be a loving Creator. "My God, my God, why have you forsaken me? Have I not serviced your altar, turned my back upon temptation, reached out to the needy, comforted the suffering?"

There is, of course, no answer, only the sound of my own plaintive voice, echoing hollowly in the empty room . . . in the emptiness of my soul.

I rail against the healthiness of my body, the soundness of my mind, condemning me to survival, left to the cruel emotions I had, until now, so carefully locked away.

# OUR CHRISTMAS ANGEL

The urgent jangle of the telephone claws its way into the soft cocoon of my sleep. Groggily, I reach across to the bedside table and lift the annoying instrument from its station.

"Mom!" Although the frantic words crowding into my ear are distorted with anguish and fear, I recognize the voice of my daughter-in-law who I'd left at the hospital only a few short hours ago. "Mom, there's something wrong with the baby!"

My brain struggles through the cloying sludge of lingering sleep. Something's wrong with the baby—little Charles Michael, not yet twenty-four hours old? I switch on the bedside lamp, as if her words might make more sense once removed from darkness.

"What do you mean?" I push the words past a sudden tightening in my throat. "What's wrong, Linda?"

"I don't know. I don't know." She is sobbing now.

"I'll be there as quickly as I can, Hon.." I'm already reaching for the jeans and sweater I'd shed earlier. Snatching up my purse and car keys, I jam my feet into a pair of sneakers and am out the door before the phone barely settles into its cradle.

My fingers tighten on the steering wheel as I careen onto the freeway, hardly aware of my foot pressing heavily onto the gas pedal. This can't be happening again, I agonize. Unwelcome images splash across the reluctant canvas of my mind, resurrecting memories of the trauma surrounding the birth of my own first-born. Once again I am trying to assimilate the words of the somber-faced nun hovering at the foot of my bed.

"You need to be aware your baby is having some problems," she'd cautioned softly.

"She'll be okay, won't she?" Though frightened, I'd felt certain my baby girl would be all right.

"It doesn't look good, my dear." In spite of her gentle warning, I was still shocked when, a few hours later, I was told, in spite of their efforts, Jeanne Marie had slipped away.

Now, focusing on the highway ahead, I push the memory from me. That had been 1951. This was 1985. Medicine has advanced since then. Charles Michael is going to be all right. But, what if . . .? Negative thoughts nibble at the edge of my resolve. Could I be strong enough for my son and his wife if something did go wrong? It had only been six months since I'd lost my husband to cancer, and only four months before that, my nephew. Had there been time enough to build up the reserve of strength I'd need?

I wheel into a parking space and, not even pausing to lock the car, sprint across the hospital parking lot. I burst into the foyer, fume with impatience as the elevator inches its way up to the third floor where I find Linda too distraught to communicate with me. Her nurse directs me to the waiting room where, impatiently awaiting the appearance of the doctor, I perch upon the edge of my chair, my sneakers nervously scuffing the floor beneath me, my thoughts flailing helplessly at the unknown.

Surely it couldn't be anything too serious. Charles Michael seemed fine when I'd held him this afternoon. A smile eases my worried frown as I recall, several hours before, being ushered into a small room, the placard on its door identifying it as "The Grandma Room", where I was ceremoniously seated in an old fashioned rocking chair. What a lovely innovation I'd thought as I looked down at the red-faced infant placed in my arms. He looked quite debonnaire, I decided, in his jaunty baby blue stocking cap— also something new since my birthing days.

"So, Charles Michael," I'd greeted my sleepy companion. "At last we meet." He responded with an indifferent yawn. "It's good for us to have this time to get acquainted," I'd persevered. "You know, things might be a little rough at first," I cautioned, thinking of the gremlins of discontent chipping at the marriage of my son and his wife. "But, I'll be here," I promised. "Together, you and I, we'll tough it out, okay?"

My hours-old grandson wrapped his little hand around my finger, and with stoic nonchalance, pursed his tiny lips and, to my delight, emitted a series of perfect, little round bubbles.

My reverie is interrupted by the appearance of Linda's doctor. Hunching forward in the chair opposite me, he carefully explains that Charles Michael has been born with a hole in the left ventricle of his heart. It must be closed in order to save his life.

Modern medicine, modern miracles, I reassure myself. Still, "He'll be okay; won't he," I hear myself prompting.

The doctor hesitates. "I'm sorry," he apologizes. "It doesn't look good."

For the next two hours, I stand, my face pressed against the little glass window of the surgery room where three men huddle together, their white smocked forms obliterating the tiny body I knew lay on the long white table between them

+     +     +

It was a small group, maybe only five or six of us, gathering at Mt. View Cemetery that morning. It was December 24th; Christmas Eve. We were there to say our last goodbye to little Charles Michael. As we joined hands around that tiny mound of earth, I couldn't help wonder, had I frightened the little fellow away with my dire prediction of his future on this earth? Or had the Lord looked down upon this small defenseless child he'd placed in our dysfunctional midst and simply changed His mind?

Comforting me is the thought that somewhere, in a place beyond our concept, a man in a rocking chair smiles down at the baby in his arms, while Charles Michael, pursing his tiny lips, blows perfect, little round bubbles for his grandpa.

# A TIME TO FORGIVE

It felt as if a hundred tiny arrows were pricking her leg. Worse than that, she couldn't feel her foot at all. She wanted to wiggle her toes, just to make sure they were still there, but eleven-year-old Marcie knew she didn't dare. The slightest movement might awaken her father whose heavy, even breathing she could hear just beyond the mound of blankets rising like a crumpled mountain between them. Cautiously scrunching her head sideways on her pillow, Marcie could see his sleeping form stretched across the foot of the bed, the arm he'd carelessly thrown across her ankle now cutting off circulation to her foot. From the light in the hall, she could see his face, usually so dark and handsome, now pale, etched with lines of weariness. Marcie swallowed against the sudden ache in her throat.

From downstairs came the sound of her mother, softly crooning as she sought to quiet the sobs of baby Nick. Marcie glanced at the sleeping form of her sister, Beth, lying beside her, moist tears still clinging to her cheeks. Marcie knew she dared not awaken her father.

Earlier that evening, they lay very quiet in their bed, Marcie and her sister; two frightened little girls, listening to the quarrelling downstairs. There were times, in the past, when they knew their parents were angry with each other, either speaking very politely to one another—or not at all. But they'd not seen them angry as they were tonight, saying cruel, unkind things Marcie just knew they couldn't mean.

"I really don't care what you think anymore." Mama was crying.

"If that's the way you feel, maybe I should just leave!" Daddy's voice was harsh, threatening.

"Maybe you should."

Fear snatched away her breath. "Oh, please, dear God," Marcie prayed into her pillow. "Don't let Daddy go away."

Then, she heard her father climbing the stairs, the steps creaking as only they did beneath his tread. A quick glance at her sister told her Beth still slept, so Marcie lay very still, hoping her father would think she, too, was asleep. Peeking through her eyelashes, Marcie saw him pause beside the bed for a moment, felt the springs sag as he lowered himself onto its surface. Daddy's breathing sounded funny, she thought, sort of shaky, like maybe he was crying. Then, he, too, had fallen asleep. *He's just tired*, Marcie reasoned. *In the morning, he'll remember we love him and everything will be all right again.* If only her leg would stop tingling.

A sharp arrow of pain twanged across her ankle—Marcie's leg jerked involuntarily. At the foot of the bed, her father stirred, then sat up. Marcie heard his heavy sigh, felt the bed shift as he rose to his feet. She struggled against the urge to open her eyes in the silence that followed.

Then, "Good night, my angels," came her father's husky whisper. His large frame was silhouetted in the doorway and the stairs were creaking again beneath his weight. Moments later, voices drifted from the rooms below . . . hostile, unfriendly voices.

Angrily, Marcie jabbed her right heel into the numbness of her left foot. "It's all your fault," she hissed. A thousand tiny pinpricks stabbed at her toes, shot up her leg. Grateful for the excuse of pain, she turned her face to the wall and let the tears come.

+       +       +

The morning sun, filtering through the big maple tree outside the bedroom window, awakened Marcie. She lay still for a moment, watching the leafy patterns dancing on the bedroom wall, wondering at the strange uneasiness she felt. Then, she remembered. Quickly, she sat up; she glanced toward the empty pillow beside her and then to where Beth stood in front of the dressing table, brushing her hair, her eyes still red and puffy from last night's tears. Hopping from the bed, Marcie hurried to her sister's side.

"Are they up yet?" she whispered.

"Yes," Beth answered softly. "I heard them talking downstairs."

Together, the two girls crept down the stairway. The voices coming from the sunroom were quiet, impersonal, but to Marcie's relief, no longer angry.

"Maybe they've made up." Beth's expression was hopeful.

"You think?" After last night, Marcie wasn't so sure.

Beth's face brightened. "Let's fix breakfast for them," she offered. Not waiting for a response, she darted off toward the kitchen.

Marcie hovered uneasily in the middle of the room, glancing helplessly about at its pristine ambiance of scrubbed tile, crisply starched curtains and orderly countertops. She felt awkward here in Mama's kitchen. It was Beth, being the oldest, who helped Mama with the cooking, while the extent of Marcie's duties consisted of merely drying the dishes. This arrangement suited Marcie just fine. She could find more interesting activities outdoors, like climbing trees, or helping Daddy in the garden. Today, while her sister set about preparing a breakfast of toast, corn flakes and coffee, Marcie busied herself arranging a tray with silverware, sugar and cream, and as a final touch, the vase from the windowsill containing a rose from Mama's garden—Daddy's favorite yellow rose.

Balancing the laden tray, Marcie waited as Beth timidly tapped at the door to the sunroom. Inside, the voices paused. It was a moment before they heard Mama's light footsteps crossing the room. Her small figure framed in the open doorway, their mother stared silently her daughters and the tray they held between them.

"Come in, girls," she finally sighed. "Daddy and I want to talk to you."

"Is everything going to be okay?" Marcie whispered as Mama lifted the tray from her hands.

Their mother turned quickly away, and, eyes carefully averted, deposited the breakfast offering on the desk beside their father. Marcie stared in confusion at the two most important people in her life, behaving now like total strangers. Huddled on the couch beside her sister, Marcie listened in frightened disbelief as Daddy, his hip balanced upon the edge of the desk, nervously explained to the yellow rose in its vase, he and Mama were getting a divorce.

+       +       +

Marcie scrubbed angrily at the tiny bit of egg yolk clinging to the plate she was drying. Ordinarily, she would have popped the dish back into the sink, triumphant at discovering her sister's carelessness, but not today. Marcie glanced at Beth, then looked quickly away, not wanting to witness the tear that dropped into the soapy dishwater. Today, Daddy was moving into an apartment in town; he was upstairs this very minute, packing his things. She couldn't imagine not seeing him across the breakfast table every morning, sharing dinner every night. And yet, tomorrow, Mama would file for divorce.

Divorce. Like the cloying unpleasantness of a dose of castor oil, the word left a sickening aftertaste clinging to the back of Marcie's tongue. Nobody in her world was divorced, except maybe Frances' mother. Marcie thought of Frances, the new girl in her class at school . . . shy, quiet, with beautiful long blonde curls—but no friends. Marcie wondered now if maybe it was because Frances' mother was divorced. Then the terrible thought occurred to her, would she lose her friends when her mother was divorced?

Her doleful misgivings were interrupted by the sound of her father's footsteps on the stairs. In the next instant, he was in the kitchen, hugging her and Beth, and, with tears in his eyes, telling them to be good girls. Then he was gone. Marcie followed him as far as the door; saw him climb into his pickup and still couldn't believe it was really happening. She turned to where her mother sat, her face hidden behind a magazine clutched in her hands.

"Mama!" Marcie pleaded.

But Mama sat very still in her chair, staring at the shiny printed pages before her and Marcie knew her mother wasn't even going to try to stop Daddy from leaving. Whirling, Marcie fled up the stairway to the bedroom she shared with her sister. For a very long time, she sat on the edge of her bed, staring, unseeing, at the blank, comfortless wall, anger and frustration churning inside her. Then, slowly, deliberately, she took her diary from its drawer. *"Mama is divorcing Daddy,"* the little girl wrote across its pages. *"And I shall never, never forgive her."*

+           +           +

Reverend Matthews stepped into the pulpit to begin his weekly sermon. Marcie slumped down in the hard, wooden, church pew. This was the last place she wanted to be this Sunday morning. She was certain, by now, everyone in town knew about Mama and Daddy; knew they were getting a divorce. A few moments earlier, sullenly following her mother, sister and baby brother as they filed into their seats, Marcie saw Mrs. Andrews pause as she groped for the car keys her baby tossed into the next pew, and Marcie was certain it was to stare at them. Mrs. Duncan, clumsily struggling to separate her unruly twins, hesitated, then seemed to draw the children closer to her. Della Myers, secretly holding her boyfriend's hand, peered over her shoulder then whispered into his ear. That gossipy Mrs. Pettit glowered at them from beneath furrowed brows. Defiantly, Marcie glared back at her. It was obvious to Marcie everyone was watching them.

Attempting to scrunch further down in her seat, she cast a furtive glance around the room. That's when she saw Daddy. He looked so lonesome sitting by himself, Marcie thought. His face was thinner, and he didn't seem as tall. Suddenly, Marcie wished she were sitting beside him, longed for the comforting security of his arm around her. She half rose in her seat.

In the next startling instant, her painful agony over prying eyes, her longing desire for the nearness of her father vanished, snatched away by the Reverend's words.

"The subject of my sermon today," he announced softly, "will be 'Forgiveness.'"

Marcie sank back in her seat; her mouth dropped open. *Had he seen her diary?*

"How quickly we react to what we consider an injustice to ourselves; how eager we are to judge others."

*Was he looking right at her?*

"Have we thought to examine our own lives? Has there been no time when you have committed a thoughtless act, failed to offer kindness or compassion to another in their time of stress?"

Each word was an arrow, piercing Marcie's armor of self-righteousness, allowing tiny germs of doubt to seep in and feed her blossoming guilt. Parading before her was the memory of the times she could have been nicer to Beth, and maybe even Frances. But leading the parade of recriminations was that page in her diary, its words of condemnation glowing scarlet in her mind. From the corner of her eye, she glanced toward Mama. For the first time, she noticed the dark circles beneath her mother's eyes, the tired lines around her mouth. All at once, Mama seemed so very frail, so unhappy.

"At his darkest hour, Christ forgave." Reverend Matthew's voice grew soft. "Can't you?"

With a start, Marcie realized the services were over, everyone was standing to sing the final hymn. Jumping to her feet, she felt the tears crowding behind her eyelids. Quietly, she slipped her hand into Mama's, glanced up when she felt her mother's fingers tighten about her own. Mama's eyes were wet, like she wanted to cry, but her lips were smiling.

Marcie glanced quickly across the room to where her father turned toward them, his lips forming that sad little smile he sometimes wore when he told Mama "I'm sorry." Marcie wasn't sure she'd ever understand grownups, but of one thing she was sure. As soon as she got home, there were some changes she was going to make in her diary.

# EX ARCHE

(In the Beginning)

*Everyone has something to Fear, to Hide, to Prove.*
*To protect itself, True Self often takes Refuge behind False Self*

In the beginning was the Word. In the end was the Word. And that Word was final. It always belonged to Nigel.

In the beginning, it had mattered little to Della . . . this need of Nigel's to always have the final say. She was in love, hopelessly in love—in the beginning.

Della was barely nineteen when she landed the coveted job at corporate headquarters. While it was only a position in customer service, to Della, only recently graduated from high school, it was an exiting admission into the world of big business. Though her duties demanded little responsibility, she was still required to attend job orientation classes, needed to learn the 'nuts and bolts' of the company. That's where she met Nigel. He was the class instructor. With his bronzed complexion and hazel-flecked eyes, he was, Della thought, extremely handsome, warm, friendly, quick of wit, terribly, terribly smart and, she learned, twelve years older than she. It was love at first sight for Della.

It was impossible Nigel not pick up on the vibes Della radiated. They soon became friends, then lovers, and inevitably, husband and wife. Della spent the next two years in a hazy cloud of happiness, married to her "perfect man," the man of her dreams.

Then, Nigel began to change. Subtle little nuances shadowed his usually gentle nature. He became moody, grew impatient with Della for no apparent reason. He began to criticize her appearance, the style of her hair, the choice of her wardrobe. He ridiculed her opinions, not just at home, but when they were in public, in front of their friends. Though it was supposedly done in the spirit of teasing, Della was hurt, but she said nothing. She was still very much in love. But a whisper of dissention had begun to sigh about the edges of their relationship.

Della had long since drifted away from her girlhood friends. Now, gradually, she began to decline luncheon invitations from the wives of Nigel's friends who, seeming so much more sophisticated than she, left her feeling dowdy and plain. More and more often, she feigned illness rather than accompanying Nigel on his social engagements where, having so little in common with his associates, she frequently found herself sitting alone. It wasn't long before she quit her job, applying all her attention towards Nigel's comforts; cleaning his house, caring for his clothes, cooking exotic meals to please him. But, instead of being pleased, Nigel became increasingly irritable, his moods more erratic, until, one day, in a terrible outburst of anger, he accused her of becoming nothing more than a boring recluse. He wanted a divorce.

For the first time in their marriage, the last retort belonged to Della. "No!" she screamed after him as, in red-faced rage, Nigel stormed from the house. "Never! I'll never let you go!"

+          +          +

An hour later the phone call came, the paramedic telling her Nigel had collapsed at his desk; Nigel had been rushed to the hospital. Then, it was the doctor, telling her an aneurysm had ruptured in Nigel's brain; they had been unable to save him; they were sorry.

After the funeral, Della returned to their immaculate, empty house. She closed the drapes to the east windows facing across the manicured lawn to the street beyond. She pulled the blinds on the west windows overlooking the carefully tended English garden. She unplugged the phone and locked the doors. For the next few weeks, she drifted aimlessly about the darkened rooms, ignoring the overstocked pantry; the refrigerator stuffed with exotic foods for which she had no appetite. Her life had no purpose without Nigel to clean for, to cook for; telling her what to do. He had been her life.

Then came the day that wonderfully tenacious, irrepressible will-to-live broke through her shell of misery. She discovered she could not bear to remain hidden in her dark, self-imposed prison; could no longer tolerate being cooped up with the tormented soul she had become. Taking a deep breath, she opened the hall closet, reached inside and brought forth her purse, then her jacket. She looked into the hall mirror, straightened her collar; then carefully she adjusted "the face;" the face resembling one which had once been, but no longer was, hers. "The face" smiled, stiffly.

Clutching her purse, Della stepped out onto the porch. On wooden feet, she descended the steps and followed the stone pathway to the street. Head high, shoulders erect, she moved robot-like along the two blocks to the grocery store.

She said "Good morning" to the grocer. She nodded politely to the butcher. "The face" smiled, but deep inside, where the icy emptiness still gripped her heart, Della felt nothing.

But, then, perhaps it was a beginning.

# GIFT FROM THE SEA

I can tell the story now, now that it can no longer hurt them . . . now that they are beyond the censure of a curious public.

It was late in the spring before I finished cataloguing all the books, could close the doors of the little off-campus bookstore, and retire to my island beach cabin for the summer. As was my habit, I arose at daybreak my first day on the island for I loved to walk the beach during those early morning hours when gulls still feasted on unfortunate stranded crabs, and sandpipers practiced their stilted minuet with the waves.

I had chosen the longest route, one that would take me down around Albatross Cove where the old fishing pier clung tenaciously to its creaking pilings; where Pete's ancient bait and tackle shack still catered to the few tourists who visited our island. I had nearly reached the point sheltering the Cove when I saw her, standing on an outcropping of rocks. She wore only a light jacket to shield against the cold wind blowing off the water; whipping her dark hair about her face. Oblivious to my approach, she stood staring out at the turbulent waters of the sea.

It had been my intent to speak to her, but when I reached her, I swallowed the greeting forming on my lips. Tears were streaming down her face; a face so filled with grief I could only look away in embarrassment. I hurried on my way, my eyes riveted to the stretch of sand before me. I walked as far as the pier before I turned back. When again I reached the rock pile, she was gone.

Later that morning, when I was in the village, I stopped at the post office to visit with Myrtle. Village postmistress for as long as I could remember, she was also an undisputed authority on all the back-door activities of the locals. While we've never questioned her source, we knew Myrtle was aware of everything happening on the island. I learned from Myrtle that a young woman, Greta Berns, had rented Troy Adams' cottage at the end of the Cove, had even paid rent through the end of the summer. I also learned Greta had recently lost her husband and young son in a boating accident off the cape. Remembering what I had witnessed that morning, I wondered if it were wise, even healthy, for Greta to spend her summer by the sea—a sea that so recently had taken away such a huge part of her life.

While I saw Greta nearly every morning after that, she always kept her distance. On the few occasions we could not avoid passing one another, she would nod politely, if unsmilingly, to my morning greeting, and continue on her way. My heart went out to her, but it was quite obvious she did not encourage my friendship.

It all began that first week in July. An unseasonal fog crept in during the night and was slow in burning off. I was later than usual for my morning stroll and could see only a short distance through the heavy mist, so was nearly upon Greta before I saw her. She was struggling up the beach, staggering beneath the weight of something she carried in her arms. As I drew nearer, I saw it was a young seal pup.

"Oh, my dear! Whatever are you doing with that baby seal?" I spoke more sharply than I intended.

"I found it, alone on the beach," Greta panted.

"Oh, but you mustn't take it from the beach," I admonished. "The mother will come back for it. She's just out searching for food."

"No, no! She won't come back!" Greta seemed almost frantic in her denial. "She's dead! I just know it! The baby will starve!"

"Another seal will come for it, then," I insisted gently. "You must take it back."

"No, no! It will starve!" Greta's cheeks were flushed, her breathing ragged and uneven.

My better judgement warned me, arguing would not improve the situation. I could only watch helplessly as she struggled off toward the Cove with her burden.

That happened on Monday. My concern grew as days passed and she did not return to the beach. I was tempted to call upon her, or at least inquire about her at the village, but thought better of it. Then, on Friday, I saw her once again, but she was not alone—there was a young boy with her. My curiosity mingled with relief. Perhaps family had come to be with her, I decided, to help her through this difficult time. As I watched the antics of the child, running and skipping about her, I couldn't help but notice how protective she was, always keeping herself between him and the water's edge. Sadly, I thought what a good mother she must have been to that other little boy, the child she lost.

Suddenly, the child spotted me and, with a squeal of delight, darted away from her side. If he heard her urgent cries, calling him back, he did not heed them, but continued his flight until he stopped in front of me. With an inquisitive cock of his head, he gazed up at me with such beautiful, penetrating eyes, I felt my breath catch in my throat. Then, just as quickly, he darted back to Greta. But not before I noticed his hands; small delicate hands with fingers joined together by thin membranes of skin.

*       *       *

While they continued to visit the beach in the early morning hours, Greta was careful not to allow the boy near me again. I watched as they played and laughed together and, while it was pleasant to see her happy, I felt strangely uneasy. With utmost discretion, I questioned Myrtle as to whether Greta's family ever visited her. Myrtle assured me there had been no visitors to the Cove; that, in fact, Greta herself seldom came into the village.

"She must have taken up fishing," Myrtle offered. "Pete says she's been buying a lot of herring at the bait shack."

I had just about decided I would pay a visit to the Adams' cottage when, Friday night, I received a call from the mainland. My fall shipment of books had arrived earlier than anticipated. There was no choice; I had to go back, inventory them and stock them onto the shelves. Greta and her problems, whatever they might be, would have to wait.

I arose early on Saturday, wanting to get my beach prowl in before catching the ferry. I was rather surprised when, looking down the stretch of sand, I saw the figure of a man approaching me. While, during the summer months, some tourists did venture into our private cove, unlike me, few enjoyed these early morning hours. As I drew abreast of him, I nodded in greeting. He raised his gaze to meet mine and I'm sure I must have emitted an audible gasp when I found myself staring into a pair of beautiful, penetrating eyes— the likes of which I'd seen only once before, on this very beach, a few days earlier. I have no doubt but that my mouth was hanging open for he studied me with an inquisitive cock of his head, seemed about to speak, then, changing his mind, turned and continued toward the Cove.

\*         \*         \*

It was two weeks before I could return to the island again. Greta had not left my mind during all that time: Greta, the man I'd met on the beach, the little boy with the strange, membrane-joined fingers. I tried to shut out the thoughts crowding into my head; unwelcome memories of old fisherman's tales I'd heard, of Selkies—seals that could take human form and walk among the islanders. Tales, that's all they were I berated myself, tales to be spun on cold stormy nights. I was far too sensible and sophisticated to give them credence.

Nevertheless, now that I was back on the island, the need to know what was happening with Greta became a priority. I pulled on jeans and a sweatshirt and hurried down the beach. But, of course, since it was late in the day, the object of my perverse interest was nowhere to be seen. For the next two mornings, I haunted the beach, arriving early, lingering late; tramping fruitlessly up and down the sand where I had always seen her.

Finally, I could stand it no longer. I paid a visit to Myrtle. With what I hoped sounded like casual interest, I asked how the Adam's renter was getting along.

"You mean Greta?" Myrtle glanced up, then returned her attention to the stack of mail she'd been sorting. "Oh, she's gone."

"Gone? Gone where? What happened?' All remnants of discretion deserted me.

"I think there was some fellow staying with her the last couple of weeks. Must have been somebody from the mainland, wasn't nobody from around here. 'Cept, nobody on the ferry crew remembers him coming across." Myrtle continued to separate the mail into neat little piles. "Fact is, I never did see him— Pete did. Said he had to open early one morning; Jim Weber's brother wanted to get an early start on his fishing. Anyway, he sees them, Pete did, the Berns woman and this fellow, walking along the Cove. They had a little boy with them. Since he didn't recognize the guy, Pete figured he'd better check with the harbormaster at the marina. When Gary told him no new boats had tied up for the past week, he decided to keep an eye open. He says they were out on the beach, the three of them, early every morning."

Myrtle paused to scan the message side of a postcard before adding it to one of the stacks in front of her. "There was one time Pete says he saw Greta by herself," Myrtle went on. "She was sitting on the jetty, just staring out at the water, like she was waiting for someone. At first, Pete thought maybe the guy had left. But then, the next day, there they were again: Greta, the man and little boy. Pete figured the fellow must be somebody she knew pretty well . . . a couple of times he thought he saw them holding hands.

Myrtle slid from the stool and began stuffing the stacks of mail into their respective pigeonholes. "Well, when he hadn't seen them for two, maybe three days, and there were no lights in the cottage at night, he figured he'd better call Troy Adams. Troy comes over and checks out his place and, sure enough, Greta is gone. Troy figured she finally got herself straightened out and went back to the mainland . . . says island living can do that for you, you know, help you get a handle on things and get on with life."

"Perhaps he's right," I granted. Maybe the quiet serenity of the island, the tranquility of the sea, had restored purpose to Greta's life, I thought, had helped her to move on. With all my heart, I hoped it was true.

"Odd thing, though, about her clothes and stuff." Myrtle seemed to have momentarily forgotten the letters in her hand and a tiny frown flitted across her forehead. "Troy says she left a note saying as how she enjoyed the cottage and all—that she was leaving. Funny thing was, she didn't take none of her belongings with her." Myrtle's glance darted around the small office. "Another strange thing," she confided. "Matt, who runs the ferry boat, says nobody on his crew remembers seeing Greta getting on, or off, the ferry."

Myrtle leaned toward me, as if to share a choice bit of gossip. "You wanna know what I think?" Her voice was scarcely above a whisper. "You ever heard of the Selkies?"

*       *       *

*Legends of these seal/human beings abound along the shores of Ireland and Scotland where fisher folk live alongside the seals. The belief a Selkie's natural form is human is reinforced by their human-like cries and the startling human-likeness of their eyes. These lithe and seductive creatures supposedly live in an underwater world and don seal-like skins to pass from one region to another; shedding those skins when on dry land. When in human form, Selkies can often be identified by a thin membrane connecting their fingers and toes. The oldest tales suggest that to summon the handsome and charming Selkie man, a mortal woman need simply shed seven tears into the sea at high tide. But though he will romance her, no doubt even seduce her, he must eventually return to the sea, for that is his true home.*

# TODAY'S FORECAST
# SUNBREAKS

# FAMILY PHOTO

Grandpa sits to the right in his folding chair.
Grandma sits quietly beside him.
Uncle Charlie stands at the far end of the row,
Because Grandpa can't abide him.

Suzy's shedding big crocodile tears,
From her perch on Mama's lap.
Johnny's tongue disappears in his mouth,
When Papa gives him a slap.

Mabel's hair still needs some primping
Doris frets over a run in her sock.
Jack and Esther are no longer speaking,
Toddler Timmy wanders out on the dock.

The baby discovers Aunt Mary's corsage,
And is happily devouring a rose.
Pam tugs her hair down over her face,
To hide the zit on her nose.

The phone in the house is angrily ringing,
The smoke alarm's buzzing, too.
While cousin Bret has just discovered,
There's dog do all over his shoe.

The sun overhead continues to shift.
Now it shines in everyone's eyes.
The photographer aims his little black box.
"Come on now, smile, you guys."

# MADAME X

Having grown up on a farm, I quite understandably have access to more chicken stories than "you can shake a stick at." But rather than "run around like a chicken with its head cut off" trying to amass those treasures for your perusal, I have decided to share the one which is, *the* family chicken story, having been told, and retold, at every family gathering since it happened. It involved my mother.

A "California girl," pretty, fun-loving, my mother was only nineteen the summer she visited her relatives "up north." She took a summer job sorting apples in a packing shed owned by a farmer who eventually would become my father. Thirty-two years old at that time, he had settled down to managing the apple ranch left to him by his father. Having already "sown his wild oats," he was looking for a wife to share his life and bear his children.

They had little in common, this farmer and the girl from California. Yet, love, that greatest of architects, builds even the most impossible of bridges. And so, they were married.

As might be expected, ranch life proved to be a challenge for my mother, both physically and emotionally. Five feet tall, barely weighing one hundred pounds, she none-the-less tackled her new, unfamiliar duties with a determination that defied criticism. The emotional adjustment was more difficult. Animals, she learned, were not pets to be given pet names. Whether it was horses for labor, cows for milk, cattle and pigs for meat, animals were bred for one purpose. As for the chickens, they supplied eggs—or Sunday dinner.

Included in the flock of chickens squawking, scratching and flapping about the barnyard were "Banties", White Leghorns, and Rhode Island Reds. It was one Rhode Island Red catching my mother's fancy, to become her favorite. In spite of all cautioning, I'm sure Mother had a name for her. Since I wasn't privy to it, I will, for the sake of identification, refer to this chicken as Madame X.

Her cloak of lovely buff-colored feathers, worn like a royal mantle, was always fluffed and carefully preened. Red-combed head held high, her wattle swaying provocatively, she strutted and pranced about on her spindly yellow legs, obviously "queen" of the barnyard. Actually, as chickens go, I suspect she quite smashing, proof of her apparent allure being she was the top egg-producing hen in the chicken coop. Even that event became a major production, involving a great deal of throaty clucking and fluffing of feathers each time she settled herself upon the nest.

Then, dawned that terrible day, the day Madam X took sick. Mother discovered her one morning, not seated upon her nest, but huddled in the far corner of the hen-house, bedraggled feathers drooping, bright beady eyes hidden behind pale yellow eyelids, her proud head retracted into a scruff of buff-colored feathers.

It was my father who announced the death penalty. Madame X must be destroyed. Mother was crushed. Yet, it was the rule. Madame was no longer productive, and, even worse, she could possibly infect the other chickens with some fowl-related disease. Still, my mother pleaded with my father, certain she could nurse the condemned avian back to health. My marshmallow father, of course, could not deny his bride. He gave in.

And so, Madam X was removed from the presence of her peers and carefully placed into a box lined with towels and, oh yes, even a heating pad. Joining her in her cardboard quarantine were small dishes of warmed water and finely ground grain. But Madam X would not co-operate. She refused to eat, or drink, stubbornly maintaining her scrunched, no-neck stance. Occasionally, she'd blink those wrinkled eyelids, peer listlessly about the confines or her little four-sided world, then retreat, once again, into her comatose hideaway.

Finally, my father intervened. "There's no sense in beating a dead horse," was his favorite argument. "She's not going to get well. Let me get rid of her."

Even my compassionate mother realized the futility of her efforts, the need to put this poor creature out of its misery. Perhaps it was a loyalty to her ward that made her volunteer to perform the act of euthanasia herself. The following morning, as soon as my father left for the orchards, Mother grabbed her gardening trowel and, proceeding to her flower garden, carefully dug a shallow grave at the base of the yellow rose bush. Arming herself with the 22 pistol kept on the premises to ward off rattlesnakes and other unwanted varmints, Mother gently lifted Madame from her box and, carrying her outside, placed her beside the freshly dug hole.

As determined as Mother was to carry out her mission, the actual performance of the execution was nearly her undoing. Pointing the pistol at the hen, Mother turned her head and pulled the trigger, flinching at the sharp sound of the exploding shell. However, when she turned back, it was to discover Madame X, not lying in the hole as expected, but still huddled at its edge. Blinking accusingly at my mother, Madame pulled her neck ever further into her ruffled feathers and closed her eyelids.

Taking a step closer Mother once again aimed the weapon, turned her head, and fired. Undaunted, the condemned fowl remained perched beside her final resting-place. In desperation, Mother dropped to her knees, pressed the barrel of the 22 firmly against the feathered body, then, covering her eyes with her free hand, squeezed the trigger for the third time. For the third time, she turned to find Madame X stubbornly maintaining her up-right position.

Compassion gave way to frustration. With an impatient thrust of the revolver, Mother toppled the hen into the hole and scooped the loose earth in on top of her. Even compassion can be stretched only so thin.

While my father chuckled over his wife's dilemma, secretly, he was elated. He considered this a milestone for his young bride; she had met and dealt with harshness of reality. He was certain she was now on her way to finally becoming a "farmer's wife." Unfortunately, he was wrong. Mother never did adjust to farm life. The marriage eventually ended in divorce.

It was many years before my father was able to cope with his disappointment. "I should have followed my own advice," he lamented. "Never count your chicks before they've hatched."

# THE MAIN THING

Unaware of the splintered surface until she felt it cutting into her hand, Helen reached out to steady herself against the storeroom wall as the ancient ladder shifted threateningly beneath her. The surprise forcing a gasp from her lips was instantly replaced by irritation, stretching her mouth into a thin, angry line.

The very next item on her list of things to do, Helen fumed inwardly, would be the retaliatory destruction of this rickety, splay-legged excuse for a stepladder. Small wonder her father hadn't broken his neck if this overdue candidate for the junkyard was what he used when stocking shelves. Why, oh why, on God's green earth did he hang on to this relic? She knew the answer even before the question formed. Her father's rationale, "As long as it's usable, don't throw it away," was one she, unfortunately, could easily relate to. The frugal trait dictating her father's life was one he'd passed on to her. Which explained why her closets at home were stuffed with "things," things she hadn't used for years; might never use, but things she couldn't bring herself to throw away. Well, maybe, one day. But that wasn't today's main thing.

Helen hesitated, her hand still braced against the rough cedar, and a whimsical smile gentled the corners of her mouth. "The main thing." How often she'd heard that phrase during her childhood, in a time long ago, before divorce divided the family. "The main thing," she could still hear her father's deep voice declaring, "The main thing is to decide what is the main thing. Then the main thing is to keep the main thing the main thing." Helen sighed and straightened her shoulders. The main thing today, she reminded herself, was to sort through her father's earthly belongings, things no longer of any use to him, and, if necessary, ruthlessly dispose of them.

While intimidated by sheer volume, sorting through the clutter of the storeroom proved far less traumatic than yesterday's intimacy of her father's living quarters, where frayed satin blanket bindings, chipped dinnerware, warped fry pans and mismatched silverware gave painful testimony to her father's lonely, bachelor existence. Her brother, Nick, home on emergency leave, seemed less overwhelmed by the clutter greeting them. But he lived with his father before joining the Navy; was perhaps more familiar with their father's habits. However, living out of state, it was longer than Helen cared to admit since she'd visited her father. Now, she had only the legacy of regret for the years she'd let pass.

Helen brushed away the moisture gathering in the corner of her eye. That was in the irretrievable past and not the main thing today. The main thing today was closing out her father's affairs, his grocery market, his home, the storeroom. Yesterday, swallowing her heartache, Helen had chosen the challenge of his living quarters, determined to put her father's house in order for one last time. She might have succeeded had it not been for the cat.

The beautiful, longhaired creature, the color of autumn smoke, curled up on the doorstep when she and her brother, Nick arrived that morning, darted inside the moment the door opened.

"Whose cat?" Helen wondered.

"I think he goes with the store," was Nick's unexpected reply

"What? I thought Dad didn't like cats."

"He didn't," Nick agreed. "The last time I was home on leave, someone just dropped the cat off, and I guess it decided to stay. Dad said he tried to get rid of it, but I spotted him one night, putting out a saucer of tuna and milk."

Helen frowned. "What are we going to do with it? Who's going to feed it?"

"Oh, he'll survive," Nick assured her. "Cat's can pretty much take care of themselves."

"Well, that sounds like a rather heartless solution."

"Not much choice," Nick shrugged. "Unless of course . . ." he paused. "Might I mention at this point, the Navy frowns on its personnel keeping pets?"

"Now wait a minute, Nick. Andy is a pretty understanding husband, but I'm not so sure how he'd react to my bringing home a stray cat."

His familiar, impish grin transformed Nick's face into that of Helen's little brother again. He winked. "I'm sure you'll end up doing the right thing, Sis."

After that, it was as if the cat had already made the decision. He followed Helen wherever she went, ignoring her cross reprimands as he stalked across the cleaned tableware arranged on the counter, curled up on the freshly folded laundry, performed his morning toiletries from atop the carefully organized paperwork stacked upon the desk. The constancy of his interference did little to alleviate the trauma of sorting through the intimacy of her father's possessions. Helen eagerly embraced the much-welcomed reprieve when Nick volunteered to finish inside the house if she would clear out the storeroom. Helen was unprepared for the disorganized clutter greeting her.

"Where did all this stuff come from?" Helen gasped. "Did this all belong to Dad?"

"Dad used to store things for people," Nick attempted to explain. "Sometimes they were moving out of state, or into smaller quarters, and needed a place to leave their stuff— temporarily, of course. Most of them never showed up again, and you know Dad. He'd never throw anything away, especially if it belonged to someone else."

Helen soon found it much easier to be objective about other people's possessions than those of her father. Before long, she'd organized two piles; one destined for Good Will, the other for the dumpster. Now, teetering atop a shaky ladder, she scanned the shadowy recesses of the topmost shelf, satisfied she'd divested it of its treasures, when something in the far corner caught her eye. Cowering in the embrace of a dusty network of cobwebs, barely visible because of its color, was a small pink box.

Carefully, Helen raised herself on tiptoes, gripping the rough edge of the shelf. The ladder rocked crazily for a moment, then settled back into its lop-sided stance. Stretching her hand across the shelf's span, Helen pulled the box toward her, batting away its dusty shroud. Clutching her discovery in one hand, she clung to the rough cedar with the other, while her foot searched cautiously for the ladder's lower step. Instead of the firm surface she expected, the toe of her shoe met a soft, furry substance, a substance that immediately shot out from under her foot, leaving Helen dangling precariously from a wildly wobbling ladder.

"That darned cat!" Helen hissed. "I swear, a body'd be safer in mine field."

She peered over her shoulder in time to see its accusing glare before the large gray cat turned, and, with a defiant flick of the tail arched over his back, stalked haughtily to the opposite side of the store room. Successfully completing her descent from the ladder without injury, Helen cast an angry glance to where the cat, his back to her, perched on the edge of a packing crate.

Refocusing her attention upon the box in her hand, Helen swiped the layer of dust from its top with the sleeve of her sweatshirt. It appeared to be an old candy box, its once bright fuschia color, now faded into a soft shade of pale rose. Slowly, almost apprehensively, Helen lifted the lid. The first thing she saw, captured in the embrace of a slender strand of faded blue ribbon, was a silky lock of auburn hair. Beneath it lay a lacy white valentine. Two lovers kissed beneath the red embossed heart on its cover. The simple verse inside read, "Be Mine." There was no signature, only the scrawled message, "I love you."

Searching further, Helen discovered two ticket stubs for a stage show at the Music Hall, a carefully folded napkin with the printed logo of Harbor Lights Restaurant identifying its origin.

A frown dug furrows across Helen's forehead. Who did these mementos belong to, surely not to her father? The handwriting inside the card resembled neither that of her father, or her mother. The lock of auburn hair . . . her father had been a brunette. Helen tried to remember her mother before the early graying of her hair. Impatiently, Helen brushed aside the annoying questions invading her thoughts. Obviously, she concluded, someone left this box with her father for safekeeping, someone who surely intended to reclaim it. Then, why hadn't they . . .unless they no longer existed?

Helen shrugged her shoulders. In any case, it was of no value to her, or her brother. Restoring the treasures to their nest, she replaced the lid and turned toward her pile of discards. But, for some reason, her fingers refused to release the little pink box. What was wrong with her? This box of mementos meant nothing to her. An unexplained tightness crowded into her throat. At one time, it meant something to someone. For somebody, it held memories of a loved one, was all, perhaps that remained of a sweet, romantic interlude.

Against the wall of the storeroom stood an old steamer trunk, which, Helen discovered earlier, held an assortment of her father's personal belongings. While most of them were of little or no value, Helen could not bring herself to toss them away —not just yet, anyway. For awhile longer, she needed them to help keep her father's memory alive. Lifting the trunk lid, she gently placed the faded candy box next to a tightly bound bundle containing every letter she'd written her father over the past ten years. A streak of grime slashed across her face as she swiped at an errant tear with the dusty sleeve of her sweatshirt.

Helen felt a soft pressure at her ankle and glanced down to where the smoky, gray cat, having decided to forgive her, arched his back against her leg. Absently, she reached down to scratch behind one pointy ear. Gazing at the little pink box nestled among her father's keepsakes Helen was filled with a strange sense of peace. She felt as if, somehow, she was doing the right thing.

And that was, after all, the main thing, wasn't it?

# THE MAGIC OF CHRISTMAS

The night air was cold and crisp. Glittering stars all but snapped in the clear December sky. Icy snow crunched beneath our booted feet as we placed them carefully inside our father's larger footprints, following him across the barnyard toward the weathered building housing the farm animals. Beneath warm layers of coats and scarves, our young hearts beat joyfully, for this was truly a special evening. Not only was it Christmas Eve, but for the first time I could remember, we were being allowed to accompany Daddy to the barn at milking time.

Only a few moments before, my sister, my brother and I had been prancing impatiently about the kitchen, worrying our mother over the anticipated arrival of that jolly old man from the North Pole. Then, unexpectedly, Daddy suggested we go down to the barn with him while he milked the cows and maybe, just maybe, this would be the night the animals spoke.

Since we were babes, we'd heard the story—how farm animals were given the gift of speech on Christmas Eve so, as on the night long ago, they might express their adoration of the Christ Child. If you were in the stables at just the right time, we'd been told, you might be lucky enough to hear them speak. This magical possibility far outweighed the remote chance of surprising Santa. Even more wondrous was the never-to-be-dreamed-of invitation to share in that mystical ritual of milking time, a privilege never extended to us girls.

While it was entirely permissible for us to perform countless other farm chores, it had early-on been "carved in stone" that milking cows would never become one of our duties. It was just not an activity in which proper young ladies took part. Apparently, it was the miracle of "speaking animals" that gave exception this magical Christmas Eve.

While my father and brother sequestered themselves in the privacy of a stall with one luckless bovine, my sister and I wandered about the barn. We peered intently at the moving jaws of cud-chewing cows. We furtively studied the flaccid lips of snorting horses as they flung their heads heavenward. We listened, oh-so-carefully, to the throaty clucking of restless chickens as they settled themselves among the rafters. Yet, when my father finally returned his milking stool to its hook upon the wall, we still hadn't witnessed the anticipated miracle. Shrugging his shoulders in apparent resignation, Daddy rationalized; perhaps the animals were just too uneasy in our presence. He suggested we return to the house, promising to follow when he had completed his chores.

Disappointed, we trudged silently toward the lights of the farmhouse, slowly climbed the porch steps and pushed open the door. In startled surprise, we stared at the agitated figure greeting us, her eyes wide with excitement. In one hand, Mother held the empty plate we'd filled earlier with cookies for Santa, while the other clutched a glass, a clinging white film the only reminder of the milk it once held.

"Did you see him?" she demanded breathlessly. "Did you see Santa?" Then, "Listen," she ordered, cocking her head to one side. "Did you hear that?"

Indeed, we did hear it, the unmistakable jingle of sleigh bells, retreating around the corner of the house. In the next instant, my father burst through the door behind us. "He's here!" he panted, strangely out of breath. "But he's leaving. Hurry!" he urged. "We might still catch him."

Following our father's retreating figure, we dashed eagerly into the darkness. "Where," we pleaded, our eyes probing the star-studded sky. "Where is he?"

"Oh, he's gone." Daddy's voice mirrored his disappointment. "You've missed him."

"No," I argued, pointing to an imagined light on the far-off horizon. "I think I see him."

"I see him, too," insisted my sister. "I see him."

We were in the midst of the Depression, yet my sister, brother and I were not aware of it. Beneath our gaily-decorated tree lay all the treasures our little world could offer. A hand-sewn wardrobe awaited the Shirley Temple doll my sister had received the Christmas before. My beloved two-year-old baby doll nestled in a newly painted cradle. For my brother, there was a bright red Radio-Flyer. Oranges, apples, nuts and homemade candies spilled from dishes once standing empty on the dining room table. It was a wondrous sight to behold!

"Too bad we missed Santa," Daddy apologized. "But we'll catch that old guy next year."

My friend at school said there was no Santa, that he was only make-believe. But when I looked up into Daddy's twinkling eyes, I knew my friend was wrong.

Next Christmas Eve, we would surely catch that glimpse of Santa before he dashed out of sight. And who knows, if we're very quiet when we go down to the barn, maybe, just maybe, next year we'll hear the animals speak.

# THE OLD HOMESTEAD

She was already old when I was born, her unpainted siding darkened from exposure to countless hot summer suns and freezing snows of as many winters. A regal dowager, indifferent to the ugliness of her boxy, two-story frame, she haughtily defied the elements, as indestructible as the pioneers who created her. Flanked by two drooping willows, a gnarled apple tree and a towering evergreen, she held court from her position in the center of the valley. On the sloping canyon walls surrounding her, tall, dignified pines nodded and sighed, like weary, indulgent parents, as constant capricious air currents cavorted among their branches.

Icy, cold water was piped, unfiltered, to the kitchen sink from an artesian spring nestled in a lush grove of willows and reeds at the head of the canyon. Overflow from the spring gurgled down the valley floor, edged quietly past the barnyard where it was temporarily diverted into a watering trough for the livestock. Spilling back into a stream, it bubbled alongside the house, its cold waters chilling milk-filled Mason jars and an occasional summer watermelon. Finally, ambling down an incline to provide a perpetual flushing system for the outhouse, the brook ended its journey at the edge of an alfalfa field, spreading into a marshy bog beneath a grove of "money trees", their tiny flat leaves twirling and flashing like coins in the sunlight.

Beneath the old house, a root cellar had been dug into the earth. Canned fruits and vegetables, fresh carrots, potatoes and onions were stored in the dark, cave-like interior. A wooden cellar door kept foraging critters out. A single wooden plank, running along the damp earthen floor, served as a walkway and also as a deterrent to probable electrocution when the light bulb hanging overhead was switched on.

At one corner of the house, a bronze bell, suspended from a wooden crossbar, hung in readiness to summon the men from the fields at mealtime, or, in case of an emergency, its clanging would bring help from neighboring farms.

Board steps led up from the backyard onto a screened-in porch where, alongside a perpetually fermenting crock of sauerkraut, a four-legged washing machine patiently awaited Monday mornings when it would be rolled across the worn linoleum into the kitchen.

I can imagine the fear and trepidation that must have trembled through that old house on washdays, for I still remember them as fearfully exciting adventures. While a reservoir was attached to the wood-burning cook stove for the purpose of heating water, it could, by no means, supply the amount necessary to accommodate the washing for a family of five. So, large pans, filled and refilled at need, were placed atop the stove and the insatiable fire stoked from a bountifully stocked wood box at its side.

No protective insulation encased the metal stove pip escorting ash and smoke into the outside air so the roof and ceiling often became overheated. On such occasions, a specially appointed sentry stationed outside alerted those on the inside and waiting buckets would be filled at the kitchen sink.

One would-be firefighter struggled up the ladder, always positioned against the side of the house, and doused the smoking shingles, while whoever remained in the kitchen below, scooped water from either of two washtubs and flung it toward the smoldering ceiling. This was often considered the least desirable of the two stations since the combined waters had a tendency to respond to the law of gravity. Meanwhile, the evening meal of red beans simmered doggedly in a pot at the back of the stove.

Tuesdays, ironing days, proved to be not quite so traumatic. Of the previous families sheltered by the old house, the most recent had updated her with an electrical system— such as it was. Exposed, black electrical wires, held in place by an occasional white ceramic conductor, tracked their way across the yellowed ceiling to a single, bare light bulb hanging in the center of the kitchen. The ironing board was placed beneath this light and, with the iron's stretched-out cord plugged into the light socket, wrinkles were urged from clothing blown dry on outdoor clothes lines the day before. Today, tomatoes and mushrooms were added to last night's leftover beans, simmering once again on the back of the stove.

Each room in the old house carefully guarded its own individual ambience. A pot-bellied wood stove dominated the bright, cheery dining room, consuming vast amounts of fuel in exchange for the meager heat it reluctantly shared. By contrast, the rarely used parlor, faded wallpaper clinging tenaciously to rough, pine walls, seemed cold and uninviting, its small windows failing in their valiant effort to lure sunlight into the dim interior. Off the kitchen was the large master bedroom, the door on one wall opening into a dark tunnel of a stairway whose steps creaked and groaned in protest when trod upon.

At the top of the stairs were two bedrooms, one light and airy, its tall ceiling-to-floor windows bedecked with lacy white curtains, the other . . . dark and foreboding, a place where nightmares were spawned. Used mostly for storage, that room's back wall carried the charred scars of an earlier fire—perhaps from a Monday washday.

It was the kitchen that was the heart of the old house, the place where she lovingly gathered her brood amid Wednesday smells of freshly-baked bread, Sunday's fried chicken and blackberry cobbler; Saturday sounds of butter being churned, the screen door slamming and giggling children hovering about the kitchen table. It was in this room where caustic odors of pine soap and lye mingled with the early smell of rain to herald the approach of spring; where summer fragrances of fresh lilac and honeysuckle drifted through open windows. Autumn beaded those walls with moisture from steaming jars packed with September's harvest, while the musty odors of winter's damp mittens and wooly hats crowded around the kitchen stove, sharing its warmth with wet puppies and sleepy children . . . all zealously guarded by that homely, aging matriarch.

The last time I saw her, the old house had begun to show her age. Stark in her aloneness, she stood in the midst of an overgrown yard, her only companion a solitary willow tree hunched over the eternally bubbling creek. No longer did anyone seek the shelter of her protective walls, now housing only a few bales of moldering hay. The glass had long since disappeared from windows that stared like sad, sightless eyes onto the tangle of untended lilacs and roses. Her siding had bleached to a colorless gray, and, as I gazed upon her from the roadway, the shingles on her roof, worn thin and wispy, fluttered in the ever-playful breeze. For a moment, I fancied she waved to me. I lifted my hand in response, then turned quickly away so she might not witness the moisture gathering in my eyes. For I knew this would be the last time I would see this indomitable old lady, guardian of my childhood.

A developer, the townspeople had said—a developer had purchased the land. Tomorrow, the old house would be torn down.

# TODAY'S FORECAST
# HEAVY RAINS

# WINDS OF CHANCE OR DESTINY

Was it the Winds of Chance or Destiny that plucked the weightless down from Fate's thistle, randomly scattering—or deftly guiding the soft, white-tufted seed of happiness drifting into my space?

I am lifted on wings of ecstasy; reveling in the boundless glories of flight as, like two kindred spirits, we glide and float upon the ever-changing currents.

My soul would sing
With the joyful delight of sharing
My heart could burst
With the gentle beauty of caring

Then, suddenly, without warning, the capricious winds shift, swooping between us, tearing us apart. Like a wounded bird, my soul plummets to earth - its broken wings fluttering feebly . . .futilely, and I am left alone, to face my bleak destiny of eternal night.

Yet, it is not the darkness
That robs me of sleep
But the absence of light
For which I weep.

# FIRST LOVE

We'd known each other almost forever, you and I, practically grown up together. I remember the first day you came into Miss Clayton's third grade class. You were new in town, she told us, and needed our friendship. You looked anything but needy as you stood glowering at us from the doorway. Even your thick, black hair, springing from your scalp in every direction, seemed to reflect the defiance in your dark eyes.

When Miss Clayton directed you to the vacant seat behind me, I turned to smile my welcome. But you drew your dark eyebrows together in a ferocious frown, crossed your eyes and twisted your lips into a grotesque grimace. I stuck out my tongue and vowed if you never had any friends, it would certainly be no concern of mine.

From that day on, you set about making my life miserable. You untied my hair ribbons, stole my ruler, broke the lead tips off my pencils and constantly kicked the bottom of my chair. One day, it became too much. When you pulled my hair for what must have been the hundredth time, I lost my cool. Turning, I grabbed a healthy handful of your dark hair and yanked as hard as I could. My temper tantrum passed quickly and I was suddenly overcome with embarrassment.

Red-faced, I turned toward Miss Clayton, expecting a severe reprimand. To my surprise, our teacher didn't even look up from her desk, but continued correcting papers as if she hadn't seen what just transpired— though I knew she had. I glanced back toward you and was amazed by the wide grin of awe and admiration covering your face.

That was the turning point. From then on, while we weren't exactly friends, we no longer were enemies.

By the time we were in Mr. Robert's fifth grade class, we were walking home from school together. When we reached our seventh year, you were carrying my books between classes. I guess, by then, I would have admitted to our friendship.

You were definitely a part of my life during junior high. You played Romeo to my Juliet in the high school play. We did our studying together; you were a whiz at math and helped me pass algebra and geometry. You went on to trigonometry, but I decided to quit while I was ahead.

You were so proud of your first car, a black Ford coupe with the rumble seat wired shut. I was the first one you gave a ride to and I spilled my cola all over the upholstery. I thought sure you'd yell at me.

But you didn't.

We never really dated, but always seemed to end up with the same crowd at basketball and football games. You asked me to go to the Homecoming Dance and I said I would. But, then I broke our date and went, instead, with the high school football star. I was sure you'd dump me after that.

But you didn't.

It didn't surprise me when you were among the first to join the service when the war broke out. It did surprise me when the night before you left you came to say goodbye and brought me a little white box with a gold locket inside. "A friendship token" you called it. I tucked it away in the back of my dresser drawer, certain you'd forget me once you were away.

But you didn't.

From everywhere you went you sent me letters, some cheery and funny, some wistful and melancholy. I began to realize how much I missed you, how much you meant to me and decided I'd tell you so when you came home.

But you didn't.

All I had left that was you was a shiny gold locket in a little white box tucked away and forgotten in the back of my dresser drawer. I buried you in the garden in a grave, tiny as an open hand, and patted the earth firmly back into place.

I would like to say, one day, to my surprise, a little flower sprouted from that corner of my garden; that I built a little fence around it and watered it faithfully every day. But that would not be so. The grass has grown over that spot and it looks no different now than the rest of the yard.

I built no shrine to remind me of you, but when I smile at the woman sitting by herself on a park bench, nod at the man walking the boardwalk alone, or when I tell a friend, "I love you," it's then I remember you.

# THE SMILES WE LEFT BEHIND

Overnight bag still suspended from my fingers I paused in the center of the hotel room, waiting for my eyes to adjust to its shadowy interior. The bed and nightstand were but dark images, barely discernable in the fading evening light filtering through partially closed blinds. It was seven-thirty, much later than I planned on beginning what was to be my weekend get-away to Vancouver, a place I'd avoided for so many years. But blustery weather and rude traffic fought me all the way north from Seattle. Weary, eager to be off the road, I stopped at the first hotel I came to on the outskirts of town. In spite of my fatigue, I was aware of an odd familiarity about the ugly edifice. I ignored the strange uneasiness nipping at the edge of my sub-conscious. One of a hotel chain, it was quite natural it might resemble its counterparts.

Dropping my luggage onto the bed's surface, I fumbled for the switch to activate the bedside lamp. My fingers closed about the knob's serrated surface and though its click was clearly audible, no light was forthcoming. Exploring further, my hand encountered an empty light socket. I smiled to myself. It would seem the "bulb bandit" had struck again. The smile was driven from my lips by the sudden knot fisting itself in my chest. Whatever had brought that phrase to mind? What cruel trick was Fate playing?

I felt the hairs prickle at the nape of my neck. Cautiously avoiding the minefield of wrinkled carpeting snatching greedily at my spike-heeled shoes, I groped my way across the dark room to a floor lamp I somehow knew would be there. A twist of its switch and the room was bathed in the watery light of a low wattage bulb. I glanced uneasily about that strangely familiar room. It had changed little, if at all. A little shabbier, perhaps, but the same drab wallpaper clung to the walls. Ghostly memories crowded around me, prodding, whispering, ruthlessly demanding to be recognized.

*     *     *

Once again, it is my husband and I, standing in the middle of this room, illuminated then, as now, by the dim bulb of the floor lamp. Whether by plan, or by chance, there were no light bulbs in any of the lamps save the fifteen-watt bulb in the floor lamp. I suggested it was a ploy to conserve electricity. My playful spouse insisted it was the work of a phantom bulb bandit.

That spontaneous weekend to British Columbia turned into near frustration. Unaware of the convention filling all available hotels, we hadn't made advance reservations. It was nearly eight o'clock before we found a vacancy at this hotel, located in what appeared to be a somewhat questionable area on the outskirts of Vancouver. However, having identified itself as a part of a well-known hotel chain, how bad could it be, we reasoned. Pretty bad, we soon discovered.

We chose to overlook the tackiness of the lobby, the rudeness of the disk clerk and even the yellowing palm well on its way to a post-mortem state. Feeling fortunate to have at least found lodging, we decided to bite the bullet and make the best of the situation. Once our bags were unpacked, we proceeded down to the dining room where we concluded biting the bullet might have been the better option. Never having sampled exotic East Indian cuisine, the hotel chef's specialty, we were too weary to go in search of other nourishment and meekly followed the dark-haired, mocha-skinned waiter to our table. Once seated, we were provided with a menu, written, we discovered to our dismay, in Hindu or Pakistani, but with no English translation. Helplessly, we scanned the unfamiliar wording.

"Let's just get a salad," my husband suggested. "That should be safe enough."

However, when our waiter returned, we learned he knew very little English so was unable to help us order. Randomly, we pointed to a selection we assumed to be a list of salad offerings. Very shortly, our order arrived; two small bowls of a whitish sauce, each containing one tomato wedge and one slice of cucumber. It would seem we'd ordered salad dressing, nothing more.

"I can't eat this," hissed my disgruntled spouse.

"Well, what, then?" I argued, nodding toward the undecipherable menu.

The waiter was re-summoned to our table where, with a great deal of motioning and pantomiming, we were able to order bread with our meal. Of course, it was unleavened bread. With a sigh of defeat, my better half, forking the tomato wedge and cucumber slice onto the flat bread, then covered it with the sauce and rolled it into a burrito. I followed suit and we consumed what would be our evening meal.

A large, swarthy fellow, looking like something that might have escaped Aladdin's lamp, left his post at the cash register and advanced across the room to tower over our table. "You like the food?" Although his English was less than perfect, there was no doubting the challenge of his inquiry.

Under the table, I gave my husband a warning nudge with my toe. "Oh yes," he smiled. "It was delicious," he added, managing somehow to keep a straight face while I buried my giggles in the folds of my table napkin.

Back in our room, we showered and prepared for bed, hoping for a least a good night's sleep. We were scarcely settled in when we were awakened by a frightful commotion originating in the street outside our window. Leaping from the bed, my husband threw back the drapes then quickly dropped to his knees, where he remained, peering out into the night.

"What is it?" I demanded. "What's going on?"

Fingers to his lips cautioning me to silence, my till-death-do-we-part partner motioned me to his side. "You won't believe this," he whispered,

Slipping from the sheets, I crab-walked my way to the window and raised my eyes above the sill. Directly across the street from our room, brilliant hundred-watt light bulbs chased one another around a huge, equally brilliant row of lashing lights blinking their blatant invitation to *Sin City*. Milling about below the gaudy sign, a group of "sinners" had spilled into the street with their revelry. They surrounded, and were seemingly harassing, a tall, rather large, blonde woman—or was it a man? They gleefully dodged the lethal-looking umbrella swung at them. Apparently tiring of this sport, they closed their circle, and as we watched aghast, disarmed their victim and tied him, or her, to the lamppost.

Not waiting to see what might happen next, my husband snatched up the phone, and, arousing no response from the front desk, dialed the police station. At that moment, the sound of sirens filled the night air and a police car careened around the corner, screeching to a halt outside our window. *Sin City* immediately swallowed up her playful clientele while the police, having freed the hapless victim, simply drove away.

We returned to our bed, hoping to recapture what was left of the night's sleep. But there would be no sleep for us that night. The raucous sounds of merriment continued to beat at the inner walls of the *City*, periodically erupting into the street below. It was nearly eight o'clock the next morning when, gratefully turning in our key, we terminated our stay at "Insomnia Lodge." Later, we would enjoy a good chuckle, remembering the night we spent outside *Sin City*.

\*       \*       \*

Now, standing alone in the middle of the hotel room, I felt a dampness on my cheeks and realized I was weeping—weeping for the irretrievable past. Swallowing the lump at the back of my throat, I moved to the window and pulled back the drape. No bright lights greeted me from the building across the street. Only a few broken bulbs lined the once garish marquee. A tattered "Closed" sign fluttered from *Sin City's* darkened window.

I let the drape fall back into place. I knew I would not, could not, stay here the night. Lifting my still unopened bag from the bed, I switched off the lamp. Carefully making my way across the uneven carpeting, I stepped into the hall and quietly closed the door behind me. No one was at the front desk when I stopped to check out. The lobby was quiet except for the dry rustle as my bag brushed the brown brittle fronds of a dead palm. Dropping the hotel key onto the counter, I glanced at the clock on the wall. It was nearly eight o'clock.

Some memories, like some dreams, I decided, are best left behind

# AVALANCHE

Chawuk. Chawuk. The sound vibrated in the crisp morning air, bouncing from the steep mountainside as each blow of the woodcutter's axe sent light brown wood chips skittering across the crusted snow.

William stepped aside as the thick trunk of the tall fir shuddered and the tree slammed with a *thwump* into the deep snow. The ground shook with its impact, the echo ricocheting from the canyon walls. Arching his back against the brace of his hand, William drew the cold winter air into his lungs and raised his eyes to the ridge of the hill. The light of an early morning sun spilled over the crest of the mountain; slid down the trough of a ravine, reaching with pale slender fingers across the canyon floor toward the tiny cabin huddled at the base of the hill. William's gaze followed the shards of light to where his nine-year-old son, Henry, shoveled last night's accumulation of snow from atop the cabin roof. A thin wisp of smoke rose above the crude stone chimney.

A smile crept across William's face at the thought of his little family sheltered within those walls. He pictured his wife, Laura, bustling about the small kitchen, preparing breakfast for their young daughters and the Reverend Briggs, a traveling minister who spent the night with them. Even though the journey had taken them six months, his earlier decision to join the wagon train heading to the Northwest, where land was available to homesteaders, turned out to have been a good one, thought William.

He allowed himself a moment to bask in the warm glow of contentment before, once again gripping the handle of his axe, he bent to the task of stripping branches from the felled tree. He hesitated; raised his head to listen. The echo of his labors of a few moments ago, still played among the hills rising above the little valley, an echo he knew should have faded by now. Instead, the sound seemed to have grown, rolling off the hillside, surrounding him. Straightening, he glanced uneasily across the canyon toward the mountain towering above the cabin.

At first, he saw only the white blanket of snow, pinned to the hillside by spears of lean, scraggly pines. Then, the whole mountain seemed to shiver, and as he watched in mute horror, a huge slice of dirty gray ice pushed itself free from the muddy earth and began moving slowly down the hillside.

"Good Lord!" The anguished cry tore itself from his lips.

William flung the axe from him. It slammed against a tree and slithered, unheeded, across the snow as the horrified woodsman hurled himself down the mountainside. Like a jealous lover, the icy snow clutched at his ankles. He stumbled, fell, then struggled frantically to his feet again.

"Laura!" His warning cry was lost in the rumble and roar of the churning mass which, sweeping rocks and trees before it, smashed down upon his creation of log and stone, then sliding across the valley floor before finally slamming to a stop in a massive spray of ice and snow.

Stunned, William stared in disbelief at the ugly scar slashing its way across the floor of the canyon. Then, he was slipping, sliding, floundering his way to the spot where his home once stood. Flinging himself to his knees, he clawed savagely at the snow with his bare hands. The frozen crystals slashed back with icy sharpness until their battlefield tinged red with William's blood. But there was no trace of the cabin, no stone blackened by breakfast fires, no scrap of gingham which might have shaded a window, nothing more than a broken shard of blue crockery to give testimony to the warmth and happiness which was once his home. Only ice . . . and snow . . . and mud.

Emptiness as great as the silence now filling the canyon crept through William, spreading to the very tips of his fingers, draining his every last ounce of strength. His shoulders sagged; his mutilated hands fell helplessly to his sides.

"Laura," he whispered hoarsely. "Laura."

He bowed his head, surrendering to an overwhelming grief, letting the tears spill down his cheeks, when he heard it—from somewhere beneath the mountain of gritty snow surrounding him—a baby crying.

\*        \*        \*

Remembering her mother's instructions, fourteen-year-old Mary carried the blue bowls filled with breakfast oatmeal to the kitchen table, careful to place the first bowl in front of the Reverend Briggs. Rewarding her with a toothy smile, the Reverend clasped his hands and closed his eyes in preparation for the morning blessing. His eyes flew open and a scowl replaced his benevolent demeanor when, accompanied by a thunderous sound, a sudden jolt set the bowls rattling atop the table's wooden surface. Mary glanced apprehensively toward her mother.

"It's William," Mama offered the minister an apologetic smile. "He's logging trees this morning."

The Reverend responded with a tight smile of his own before, with a small, belabored sigh, he once again closed his eyes and bowed his head. Dutifully bowing her own head, Mary glanced down in time to see baby Belle, just learning to crawl, disappear beneath the kitchen table. Immediately, Mary remembered the hot stones Mama put there this morning to warm the Reverend's feet. Quickly slipping from her chair, Mary dropped to her knees and reached for the baby, only vaguely aware of the strange rumbling sound filling her ears.

\*        \*        \*

"What is your deliverance from life and death?" The Reverend's muffled voice came as if from a long distance away.

Mary struggled against the smothering weight robbing her of air. She could feel Belle's little body squirming beneath her; hear her screaming, and screaming. Cold dampness saturated the front of her dress before Mary realized the moisture came from snow being melted by the baby's angry breath. Sudden panic exploded inside her.

"Mama," she cried out in her fear, "Mama! Mama!"

The nearness of the response brought a bit of comfort. "Hush, child." Her mother's voice was calm, reassuring. "Lie quiet and breathe as lightly as possible."

Mary's head throbbed from the piercing, unrelenting screams of her little sister.

"Are you hurt?" Mama prodded gently. "Can you wriggle your arms and legs?"

"Yes, yes I can, Mama."

Mary could feel the baby thrashing beneath her, beating her protector with tiny fists.

"From whence do you know your sin and misery?" Mary was startled by the Reverend's voice, so strong at last night's Bible reading, now weak and shallow.

There was silence and then, "Mary." It was Mama again. "The first thing to know about a baby is to keep her warm and dry."

*How am I supposed to do that?* Mary wanted to cry out. *When everything around us is cold and wet?* Little Belle was howling even louder now.

"For croup, rub her chest," Mama persisted, "with a mixture of rendered mutton and turpentine."

"How are you delivered?" the Reverend asked softly.

"Mary, you can get sixty loaves of bread from a sack of flour, if you are frugal. I always could."

"Yes, Mama."

"And remember," Mama cautioned, "always seal your crock of sourdough with a layer of water. Seal your buttermilk the same way."

"But you always churn the butter, Mama," Mary countered. "My job is to milk the cow."

The woman who had given Mary life was silent for a moment, but when she spoke, Mary heard a disturbing tremor in the familiar, beloved voice. "You will have to do both now, Mary, milk the cow *and* churn the butter."

"When God calls you, you cannot fight it." The Reverend's message of submission was barely audible.

In a stronger voice, her mother continued. "Roasted barley is the best substitute for coffee; use the juice of boiled corncobs for sweetener. But don't drink it up faster than you make it," Mama cautioned.

"Dear God, have mercy upon our souls." A note of despair shadowed the minister's urgent supplication.

Tears welled into Mary's eyes. "Where is father?" she sobbed. "I want my father."

"Hush, Mary." Mama's voice was soft. "You mustn't be afraid. Your father will find us."

"But when, Mama, when will he find us?"

"I don't know, my child, but you can be sure he will find us. You will see your father again, I promise. And your brother, too," she added.

The baby was quiet now. Having cried herself out, she lay wet, but warm, beneath the protection of Mary's body. Though she shivered from the cold, Mary felt euphoric drowsiness creeping over her, tugging at her eyelids. It was Mama's sharp command startling her to wakefulness.

"Mary! You mustn't forget; if that Indian, Pokamiakan, comes to the door, hide little Belle in the breadbox."

The Reverend's voice was little more than a whisper now. "What is your only comfort in life and death?"

This time, Mama replied. "That I am not my own, that I belong to Jesus Christ."

"And from whence . . . " The Reverend's words came in tortured gasps now, "from whence . . . do you know your sin and misery?"

"From the Word of God."

This time, Mary obediently echoed her mother's response.

"And how . . . how are you delivered?"

Mary waited for her mother to answer . . . but she did not.

*        *        *

It was nearly nine hours later when, with the help of neighbors and his son, Henry, who had miraculously ridden the crest of the frightening wall of snow, William pulled Mary and Baby Belle from their cocoon of snow.

The Reverend Briggs was dead.

Mama was dead.

Splintered logs, bits of furniture, the wheel of a sewing machine and one shattered blue crockery bowl were all that was left of the little cabin once huddled at the base of the hill.

# HOUNDS OF HEAVEN

Down the shadowy corridor of his nightmare, my father flees without waking. Fevered body bathed in perspiration, ashen face contorted with fear, he struggles against unseen demons that pursue him relentlessly the darkness of his dream.

For the third night, his terrified cry has brought me rushing to his bedside. I grasp the large, bony hand clutching the tangle of sheets and wince in pain as that calloused hand grips mine with a strength I not thin remained.

"Father!" I plead. "Father! Wake up!"

It us a moment before he frees himself from the clutches of sleep, and then it is with unexpected suddenness that he raises his stiffened body upright in bed. His eyes stare into mine, unseeing.

"Father." My soft prompting reaches into the vacuum and awareness slowly returns.

He loosens his grip upon my hand. "Ah, lass, forgive me," he sighs. "I've disturbed your sleep again."

Anxiously, I watch for the color to return to his sunken cheeks. "Are you all right, Father?"

"Aye, I'm fine, lass. I'm fine." Weariness washes over his face. "'Tis the dream again. It will give me no rest."

"If you talked about it," I offer.

My father squeezes his eyelids shut, and wrinkles dig deeply into the corners of his eyes. Releasing air through pursed lips, he lets his head sag against the headboard. "'Tis the Hounds of Hell, lass. They'll not let me be."

A painful lump crowds into my throat. Gently, I arrange the coverlet about my father's frail shoulders.

"'Tis the same each night." His eyelids flutter open and his eyes, clouded with misery, fix themselves vacantly upon a spot on the ceiling. "I see her in the dream, your beautiful mother. She stands at the end of a long hallway, her arms stretched out to me. But, when I move toward her, her dear, sweet face moves farther away." A look of pain slashes across his face. "She calls out to me, 'Hurry, Thaddeus, hurry'."

Releasing my hand, which he has held until now, Father drags his gnarled knuckles across his eyes. "'Tis then I hear them," he whispers, his voice barely audible, "snarling and snapping at my heels. 'Tis a great fear I know, and I run faster and faster, but they are ever close behind me, these Hounds of Hell, eager to devour me."

He pauses to draw a deep, ragged breath. I wonder if he will go on and almost hope he doesn't; sorry I have asked him to relive the terrors of his nightmare.

But my father's voice is steadier, now. "When I awake, I remember your mother's lovely face and wonder why she would be in the same dream with these terrible beasts. The eyes he turns toward me are moist with tears. "Then it comes to me, lass. They might well be the Hounds of Heaven, sent to remind me my time is short; that I'd best be getting my house in order."

"Oh, Father, no!" The denial leaps from my lips.

"Ah, there now, Daughter," he sooths, patting my hand. "Do not distress yourself. 'Tis but a dream. Go back to your bed lest I upset you more with the frightened prattlings of a tired old man."

Tucking the coverlet tenderly beneath his chin, I lean to kiss the leathery dryness of his cheek. "Try to get some rest, Father," I urge.

"We'll talk again in the morning." Once his eyes have closed, I turn off the bedside lamp and tiptoe from the room.

I slip into my still-warm eiderdown cocoon, but my thoughts give me no rest. Why the exact same dream every night? What meaning, if any, does it hold? Hours pass before sleep finally grants me sanctuary.

The sun is well up in the morning sky when I arise. Hastily pulling on my clothes, I hurry toward the kitchen. I hesitate outside my father's room. Not wanting to disturb him, I carefully inch the door open and peek inside, only to discover there is no need for my caution.

Sometime, during the night, the gentle, loving man who was my father, has slipped away, leaving behind only the worn-out body that housed him so many years. As I gaze into that dear face, where pain and stress of illness have been replaced by the soft hint of a peaceful smile, there is no doubt in my mind, it was the Hounds of Heaven that guided him home.

# TODAY'S FORECAST
# MORE SUNBREAKS

# INVASION

"Seventy-two degrees and sunny," the weatherman chortles.

Eureka! Spring at last. Time, I decide, to "gird my loins" and do battle with the foot-high grass masquerading as my lawn.

Stepping out my door, I cringe in terror at the sight of the crowds of white-crowned dandelions nodding their morning greeting from my front yard. I scowl my displeasure, wondering just when they managed to invade the lush turf I'd wrestled into place only two, short years ago.

I wince at the thought of hundreds of tiny paratroopers poised atop each scraggly stem, gathered in readiness for the lift-off signal. I sense their eagerness to be airborne, to conquer new soil, as they stir restlessly in the playful breeze, teasing and tugging at their little white parachutes.

Unheralded, a sudden image flashes across my mind, the image of a small child, cheeks puffed fat with air, chubby little hands clutching the spindly stalk of a thistle-covered dandelion. All too willingly, my memory replays the squeal of delight as, once launched into space, the seedlings took wing, spiraling higher and higher. Once again, I recapture that rapt look of fascination as the infiltrating army of miniature invaders drifts slowly back to earth.

I turn reluctantly from my memories, back to the darkness filling my thoughts as I contemplate the unending summer's battle before me.

Then, responding to a not-to-be-denied impulse, I step into my yard, pluck a dandelion from its stem and fill my cheeks with air.

# GUILT

When I was but a little child,
Say, about two or three
I'd join my two young siblings
As they gathered at Mother's knee.

I'd listen in wide-eyed wonder
To the endless tales she told.
Of helpless maidens in distress
And knights so fealess and bold.

I marveled at the magic seeds
Growing into a stalk so tall,
That the frightful carnivorous giant
Was killed when he happened to fall.

I was oh-so-enchanted by the kissing prince,
But saddened by the princess fair.
Whose only hope for love fulfilled,
Depended on the length of her hair.

We learned how Currie tamed the mold,
Of the system invented by Bell.
How the first attempt to split the *apple*
Was introduced by a marksman named Tell.

By he time my years had reached six,
I'd decided I wanted to see
If all the stories I'd been told
Were true . . . could really be.

With the guilelss curiosity of a child,
I poked into placed forbidden.
Always seeking to make myself privy
To all that, till now, had been hidden.

Alas, the path of the inquisitive
Proved not as smooth as it seemed.
Haircutting should be left to barber,
Only Jack could harvest such beans.

Turpentine and oil will not kill weeds,
Peanut butter is not food for a fish.
Paper dolls can't be given a bath,
Elmer's won't restore a broken dish.

'Ere long I discovered, to my dismay,
Infallible I was not.
As more and more often, my sleuthing
Left me in an uncomfortable spot.

Though I stove for a look of innocence,
A thespian I could not be.
Mother somehow seemed to know,
The obvious culprit was me.

"Can you read the words on my forehead?"
I despaired from the depths of disgrace.
For Mother would always tell me,
"Guilt is written all over your face."

# MAVERICK MEMORIES

Strange, the moments that get caught in the lint trap of our memories as we tumble through this life. I'm not referring to those warm nostalgic memories so carefully folded and tucked away, the sigh, the smile, the occasional tear, memories to be brought forth and fondled whenever we choose to review the choreography of our lives. I mean those maverick memories, wafting about like orphaned children, homeless vagrants. Evoked by an unexpected sound, an elusive odor, a familiar sight, they spring from the corners of our memory banks, shimmer across the screen of our minds. Then, before we can categorize them, relegate them to their proper place in the order of our lives, they are gone, disappearing into the amnesiac vacuum from whence they came.

\*         \*         \*

A soft, gentle fragrance of perfume drifts from nowhere; Chantilly Lace, Mother's favorite. The image of my tiny, five-foot, ninety-eight pound mother flashes before me, vibrant, intense, always in a hurry. A single mom now, responsible for three youngsters, working weekdays, she dedicates her Sundays to familiarizing her children with their new surroundings. Mandatory excursions to Volunteer Park, Pike Place Market, Pioneer Square were outings we children likened to The Charge of the Light Brigade as we struggled to keep up with

our fleet-of-foot mother. There was to be no dawdling. We were on a
mission. So much to see— so little time. What year was that, the year
we moved to Seattle?

*                 *                 *

A discarded Betsy Wetsy doll, her lips pursed in anticipation of her
next feeding, lies forgotten, unwanted in the Good Will toy bin. I'm
suddenly reminded of a little girl, huddling beside a high chain link
fence, her fingers stretching through the diamond shaped wire openings
to stroke the puckered lips of a rubber Betsy Wetsy doll wedged between
an old inner tub and a stained rubber bathmat.

For weeks now, John Cameron Swayze has ended his news cast
with a plea for the American people to donate old rubber items to the
war effort—it was a way to support our fighting troops. For weeks, I
agonized and debated. Finally, one day, after feeding Betsy, changing
her one last time, then dressing her in her best nightie, I marched
down to the end of Main Street to where an enclosure had been
created to receive "war effort" donations from the patriotic. Giving
Betsy one last kiss, I took a deep breath and I tossed her over the top
of the ten-foot fencing.

The instant my cherished rubber baby doll left my fingers, I realized
the gravity of my action. Horrified, I watched as she bounced off a
stack of old rubber tires, slithered along the fence, coming to rest at my
feet, but out of reach. I visited Betsy every day during my lunch hour,
walking the short distance from the school house to crouch beside that
imprisoning closure, poking my fingers through the rigid steel mesh,
caressing Betsy's cold little face and explaining to her what we were
doing was the right thing. I remember the heartbreak of remorse and
loss the day I arrived to find the enclosure empty. Betsy was gone. How
old was I then, those early years of the war?

*                 *                 *

"Wishing can make it so." I hear the familiar refrain and once again I am at Ohme Gardens, standing before the wishing well. Clutched in my hand is the penny just given to me by my mother.

"Hurry, make your wish," she prods impatiently. "Or we'll go on without you."

What do I wish? That Mother and Daddy will reconcile their differences, that we will be a family again? How old am I now, thirteen, almost fourteen, too old to be that naïve, that unrealistic? What then do I wish for?

"Hurry," urges mother.

Overhead, a small piper cub traces lazy arcs across the sky, its bee-like drone in harmony with the warm summer day. "I wish I could be up there, in an airplane, away from everything here on earth," I whisper, and toss my penny to the mysterious, wish-granting entities residing in the deep recesses of the little well.

No more than a week later, I find myself perched upon the buddy seat of a motorcycle, headed for the Wenatchee airport. The owner of the motorcycle, a young man who works in the apple packing shed next to my mother, is also a licensed pilot. It is a windy day; once airborne, gusts of air buffet our small plane, tossing us upward— unpredictable air currants suck us down. Wind whistles through gaping seams also allowing daylight to enter the sides of the small Piper Cub. Its wings rattle and shudder as the tiny craft struggles against nature's turbulence. Finally forced to land, we discover, due to windy conditions, no other planes are being allowed to take off. Wow! What a fantastic, exciting experience. How, I wonder, could this, the unbelievable, the impossible have happened? Did the fabled denizens of the magical wishing well actually grant me my wish? Can wishing really make it so? An elusive whiff of Chantilly Lace hovers in the air.

*        *        *

The aroma of pipe tobacco; I'm sitting on my father's lap while he blows warm, soothing smoke into my infected ear. Sharp shards of pain are held in abeyance while mother coaxes the tiny flame sputtering beneath a small pan of olive oil, heating atop the kitchen's wood stove.

\*　　　　\*　　　　\*

The sound of rain, pelting the roof overhead, brings a quiet sense of comfort and peace. Outside the darkened windows of my aunt's secured-for-the-night house, I huddle in the back seat of our old Oldsmobile alongside my sleeping brother and sister. Mother and Daddy doze up front. The late night rain that lulled me to sleep has stopped. I swipe an opening across the steam clouding the car window. An early morning sun elbows its way through the tall evergreens surrounding us. Shafts of light slice through dripping tree branches, bent low beneath their heavy burden of moisture. Fragile fronds of fern, bowing toward the sodden forest floor, gently nudge the fenders of our makeshift bedroom. Even from within these cramped, stuffy quarters, I can smell the post-rain freshness of the morning, am aware of the stillness of early dawn. I've awakened before the others who still languish in sleep. I remain very, very quiet lest I disturb them. For this is my moment, my treasure, a maverick memory which will return, reminding me of a time when I felt safe and secure, a time when all in my world was right.

# JEREMIAH

His name was Jeremiah. I don't know if he could be considered a pet but he *was* a good friend of mine. The problem was, I never understood a single word he said. But, still, we shared some mighty fine times.*

You see Jeremiah was a bullfrog. He lived in a patch of pink water lilies just off the end of my dock. I never saw him from September through April but, oh my, how I looked forward to spring and summer. It was a sure sign winter was over when old Jeremiah stirred from the muddy lake bottom and took up residence, once again, in my lily patch. I looked forward to his deep-throated "ribbit" greeting me at the beginning of each day as I settled upon the patio with my morning cup of coffee.

Jeremiah had a friend, I believe she was a lady friend, who found shelter in a patch of lilies on the other side of the lake. They often conversed with one another across the morning stillness. Some days, she would swim across the lake to visit Jeremiah and then there would be two pair of bulbous eyes peering at me from beneath a cluster of flat lily pads.

But, oh, the evenings, how I looked forward to those beautiful spring evenings. Once the sun slipped into the waters off Lakota Beach, the frog community would come alive. The entire swamp to the east of me became a cacophony of courting calls; the warm night air filled with the frenzied amphibian chirping. I called it my Mirror Lake Frogernacle Choir— Jeremiah leading the bass section, of course. I left my windows open each night so as not to miss a single performance. It was a delightful way to be lulled to sleep.

Once the amphibian mating urges passed, the courting calls were stilled. Meanwhile, Jeremiah continued to cavort about my beach, kibitzing with me, peering at me from beneath the lily pads with those big, bulging orbs of his. During all the time I knew him, I only once saw him au natural. During the summer months, I left my rowboat upside down on the beach so if, on rare occasion, it should rain, I wouldn't end up with a boat full of water. (I live in Seattle, you know). On one particular warm, sunny day, I decided to take the boat out for a row around the lake. With the intent of righting the boat, I lifted the bow. I raised it to shoulder height before I saw him, Jeremiah, in all his mottled green and black glory, squatting in the cool shelter beneath the boat. He was huge, no less than the size of a dinner plate.

For lack of a better word, I will say I was startled. I let the bow slip from my fingers. No sooner had the heavy craft thudded back onto the beach when I was seized by the terrible realization the boat could have fallen upon Jeremiah, injured him, maybe even squashed him. Cautiously, fearfully, I peered beneath the gunwale of the overturned vessel. There was no sign of Jeremiah. I did not see him for two days and then, on day three, staring at me once again from the refuge of the lily pads, were those two big knobby peepers. How relieved I was, how welcome that throaty "ribbit" The world was right again.

But, nothing is forever. The population to the north erupted, and like an insidious, uncontrolled lava, it crawled toward us. Within a very short time, we were surrounded by suburbia. Building sites around the lake became scarce so enterprising contractors brought in fill dirt, eliminating the swamp to create more building lots. New homeowners complained the frogs were keeping them awake so foliage was cut back to distance the amphibian habitat. One-time apartment-dwellers, eager to enjoy the amenities of lakeside dwelling, now objected to living on a lake filled with weeds. Professionals were hired to poison the lily pads and water iris.

Jeremiah is gone now, now that my patch of water lilies no longer exists. The Mirror Lake Frogernacle Choir no longer sings me to sleep, having since been replaced by a Summer Symphony of lawnmowers, weed blowers, chain saws and power washers.

I miss Jeremiah. He was a good friend of mine. I never understood a single word he said, but we did share some mighty fine times.[*]

---

[*]    From the song "Joy to the World" by Hoyt Axton

# STU AND ME

(A Love Story)

I was thirty-two when we first met, in the very prime of my life. Stu was . . . well he was a rather tired-looking, old-before-his-time, fifty-two. I was a happily married woman, the mother of two young children. He was a neglected, somewhat faded, blue nineteen fifty-two Studebaker coupe.

The first time I saw him, he was parked, looking alone and forlorn, in the lot behind the corner service station. As the weeks passed, I became concerned over obvious neglect that left him exposed to the brutal elements of a Pacific Northwest winter. Upon learning the station owner was currently embroiled in divorce proceedings, I mentioned I was looking for a second hand car to take me to and from my job. To my surprise, his owner, with only a moment of hesitation, informed me the little blue Studebaker could be mine for the unbelievable sum of no more than twenty-five dollars. I knew very little of Stu's past; whether this sale was one of vengeance. I didn't ask. It didn't matter. The minute I slid behind the wheel, the minute he wrapped me in his blue naugahyde embrace, I knew Stu and I were meant for each other.

Outwardly, Stu may have shown painful signs of early aging, but beneath his hood he was as fit and vibrant as any young Olympian athlete. He became my loyal and trustworthy friend, my knight in shining—if somewhat faded—blue armor. There was no challenge too great for him. Cold winter mornings were defied with an instant growl from his throaty engine. Zealous gears easily conquered even the most formidable of Seattle's forty-five degree inclines. With me stationed behind the wheel, we raced giddily along paved freeways, bounced with reckless abandon across treacherous, rutted back roads. Each journey became an adventure with Stu sipping, oh-so-frugally, from the liquid sloshing about in his tank.

How does one justify warm feelings of affection for a piece of cold metal? How could anyone possibly understand unless they, too, had once felt that tug at the heartstrings, that pure joy of possession? Only then could they share my sudden rush of adrenaline each time I climbed into—but no, wait, it was more like pulling on a comfy pair of old jeans. That cozy little Studebaker would instantly become an extension of myself, anticipating my every move, responding to my slightest touch upon the steering wheel.

Unfortunately, like so many ill-fated romances, ours, while wild and oh-so-sweet, was, alas, destined to be much, much too short. Nearly two years had passed since the beginning of our affair and yet our liaison had not cooled. Eagerly, I still looked forward to our rendezvous each morning, anticipating the exciting moments we would be sharing, unaware of the gathering clouds darkening our future. While time heals, it also wounds, and with the passage of time came change— change that would eventually drive us apart.

It was nothing so dramatic as an accident, a local catastrophe, an unavoidable act of God coming between us, but the simple needs of a growing family with its demands for a roomier mode of transportation than Stu could offer with his two-seat capacity. More and more often, guilt knotting my insides, I was forced to make use of accommodations provided by a new, less stylish, family sedan. Exiled to on-street parking due to lack of garage space, Stu waited in stoic readiness for our now less frequent trysts. It was October. The rains had begun. I was faced with the painful realization Stu was as I had found him, spurned and neglected, once more at the mercy of the brutal elements of a Northwest winter. I could not—would not—subject my loyal steed to such an ignominy. Stu deserved so much better than that.

So it was, with heavy heart, I reluctantly signed the papers releasing Stu to the yearning arms of another. I chose to accept no more than the twenty-five dollar exchange that made him mine in our beginning.

There have been many automobiles in my life since then, sleeker, sportier, boasting glossy, unmarred coats of paint. But none has filled Stu's place in my heart. Stu was special. Stu was a Champion.**

---

** Car model – 1952 Studebaker Champion

# TODAY'S FORECAST
# STORM WARNINGS

# THE DARK SIDE

Miniature whirlpools eddy about my feet as I move through the gray mist hovering over the dry October beach grass. In the distance, beyond the dingy-white curtain of fog, I hear the eternal ocean, like a tireless baker, endlessly kneading the sandy shore into grainy smoothness. Silvery-gray fragments detach themselves from the cloudbanks overhead to become swooping seagulls, drifting above me, scattering the silence with their raucous sonant.

As I draw nearer the restless water, a cold misty blanket rises to wrap itself around me, like a widow's shroud, drawing me into its solitude, obliterating the world outside.

I am alone . . . remembering, you and I, sharing a foggy deserted beach another October day.

I torture myself, wondering—would it be easier to pretend you left me for another, that somewhere you are happily sharing joys that once were ours?

Or, is the finality of death much kinder, an acceptance you are no more? Can't it be enough just to know you are gone from my life?

Like a solitary line dancer, sidestepping upon the sand, a crab skitters across my path. I feel a strange kinship with this small creature that, like me, haunts this lonely beach, sans companion.

But perhaps one waits for him; here, beneath this rock, or, there, beyond that twisted pile of driftwood.

Without warning, a hungry gull swoops from oblivion and, as I watch helplessly, snatches the lone crustacean from the sand, then disappears into the swirling gray mist

I am alone, again.

# LOST DREAMS

Only a moment ago, I was curled up all snug and cozy in my old wicker rocker. Now, I stand poised at the edge of the back porch, listening to the silence that has drawn itself like a heavy curtain across the tranquility of the balmy summer evening. Overhead, stars still spatter the dark sky like glittering droplets of celestial mud, flung from the hooves of a prancing Pegasus. But, unexpectedly, the gentle sounds of the night have ceased.

I remain very still, not daring to move. Peering into the darkness, I strain my ears, hoping to recapture the alien, unfamiliar sound that, like a strumming guitar in the midst of a Beethoven symphony, interrupted my enjoyment of nature's nocturnal concert. I hear nothing. Then, gradually, timidly, the night sounds return. From the swamp nearby, chirping frogs bravely resume their frenzied serenade. From his sentry post amid the upper branches of a lofty pine, an inquisitive owl challenges my invasion of his domain.

"Who," he demands softly? "Who?"

Leafy foliage rustles with the passing of foraging night creatures. Cranky birds twitter angrily at having been disturbed, then snuggle sleepily back into their nests.

Cautiously, I lower one foot onto the top step, feel its dew covered dampness soaking through the soft sole of my slipper. Shifting my weight, I carefully lower my other foot then freeze, mid-step. Once again the night has grown quiet as nature's children withdraw behind their protective curtain of silence, leaving only that plaintive, unfamiliar sound, drifting alone upon the soft breeze, a sound that sends chills leap-frogging up my spine. For a moment, I think it sounds like—but no, I rationalize, it couldn't be. Yet, there is no mistaking the sound I hear—the sound of someone crying.

Hesitantly, I descend the remaining steps to the graveled walkway. There, apprehension and uncertainty halt my footsteps. I live alone in my little house on a seldom-traveled dead-end road. Surrounding trees and the undergrowth of a nearby swamp afford me a privacy I enjoy. But now this seclusion gives me cause for concern. Should I investigate this intrusion into my space, or go back into my house and lock the doors? I pause, aware of the crushed rock biting into my feet. Doubt and good judgement fall before the mighty, all-conquering sword of curiosity.

"Hello?" I call softly into the darkness. "Who's there?"

My faltering footsteps carry me across the driveway to the edge of the swamp where I peer uneasily into its bushy undergrowth. The sobbing has grown louder.

"Who's there?" Words born of false bravado quiver on my lips. Still, the sobbing does not stop.

Seeking courage, I draw great gulps of the cool night air into my lungs, then, with trembling hands, firmly part the bush in front of me. There, in the middle of a small clearing, crouching on her knees, is a young girl. Her face buried in her hands, she weeps inconsolably, her frail body shaking with each ragged breath. The pink flowered pinafore she wears is strangely reminiscent of one I'd worn in my childhood. Her dark hair cascades in long, shiny strands about her shoulders.

Quickly closing the distance between us, I kneel beside her. "What is it, child?" I urge, concern replacing my fear. "What's wrong? Are you lost?"

When she does not answer, I place a hand on her arm, hoping to lift her to her feet. Only then does she remove her hands from her face and raise her gaze to meet mine. The strangled cry rising in my throat remains trapped there, for I have not the breath to release it. Those wistful, hazel-flecked eyes peering at me from that tanned, oval face, now streaked with tears, are the very ones so often staring back at me from the pages of my childhood photo album. In one electrifying instant, I recognize the quiet dreamer, the defiant idealist, the tenacious young champion of impossible causes, the child that was I.

An icy fungus of fear sprouts in my chest, spreads to my arms, crawls up my neck, immobilizing my brain. A silent scream explodes inside my head. This can't be happening! There has to be an explanation! Like a drowning seaman cast into a tempestuous sea, I grasp at even the most improbable bit of flotsam. Perhaps this is the daughter lost to us so long ago. By some cruel twist of fate, she's escaped the death we though had taken her and she's come back. Would she not look like me? One last surviving shred of reason intervenes. She would be much older than this child, now kneeling before me.

Leaping to my feet, I stare down at this apparition of myself. "Who are you?" I croak. "What are you doing here? What do you want?"

A fresh torrent of tears spills from the girl's eyes, eyes so filled with sadness, I can scarcely bear to meet her gaze. "There is so little time," she sighs softly. "So little time." In the next moment, she is on her feet, darting away from me.

"Wait," I cry, suddenly filled with the terror of her leaving me. "Wait!"

The child pauses, looking back over her shoulder. "Please, hurry," she implores. "There is so little time." And then she is gone, disappearing into the tall reeds that fill the swamp.

I do not follow her, know I would not catch her, this child who was once me. It's not just the damp chill of the swamp numbing my body. On leaden feet, I stumble back to the road, along the walkway, up the steps to my back porch. Fearful my legs will not support me, I cling weakly to the railing. I am scarcely aware of the returning sounds of the night, overwhelmed with the restless questions crowding my mind, questions for which I have no answers. Why has this child from my past come to me? What is it she is trying to tell me? I cannot dispel the memory of the sadness in her eyes, and, yes, the disappointment I saw there. Have I failed this child, abandoned her dreams, let them perish along the way for the lack of nurturing? Have I become the woman the child hoped to be? Have I become the woman "I" had hoped to be? If not, who then am I?

"Who?" echoes the owl from his lofty perch, "Who?"

Wearily, I drop to my knees, bury my face in my hands and let the sobs of regret for lost dreams shudder through my body.

# THE DREAM

Struggling to escape the panic of her dream, Marge peered wildly into the terrifying darkness. She fought the smothering sensation of disorientation threatening to overwhelm her and forced her gaze to focus upon the familiar pale square of early morning light framed by her bedroom window. Her fingers, curved into rigid claws, clutched the bed sheets, damp from the perspiration bathing her trembling body; now cold and clammy against the unnatural heat of her skin.

Her breath caught in her throat and she held it there. Had she cried out in her fear? She strained to hear any sound from the room next to hers where Christy slept. A familiar ache of remorse surged through her at the thought of her twenty-year-old granddaughter, who should be attending classes as the University, but had postponed her entrance into college to spend time with her grandmother. While Marge welcomed the comfort of another warm body occupying the house, the first since Clifford's death, Christy's visit was for all the wrong reasons. Marge had no doubt her entire family, including her granddaughter, thought she was losing her mind. After last night, Marge wondered if perhaps they were right.

Marge regretted having ever told her daughter, Edna, about the dream. Except for those few traumatic weeks following her husband's death, Marge never experienced other than the usual subconscious mind sleep activity. Then, about a month ago, the dream had invaded the peace of her nights. A tall dark man descending the steps of a large, government-type building, the sleek black car approaching from the side street, generated a compelling sense of imminent danger and an urgent need to warn the man on the steps—but of what?

At first, she'd only been mildly disturbed by the dream, able to dispel it from her mind by the end of the day. But then, the dream had returned, again and again, each time with an increasing urgency as the car took on a more sinister aspect. In the dream, Marge would call out a warning as she ran toward the man, but sleep would always desert her before she could reach him. The vision had become more unsettling, doggedly following her through the day. She began staying up later and later each night, hoping exhaustion would free her from the nightmare, until her gaunt, hollow-eyed features aroused Edna's concern. So, Marge told her about the dream.

"Hey, Mom, Sally and I were wondering if you'd like to come spend a few weeks with us." That transparent invitation from her son Eric whose, wife made little effort to encourage anything more than a polite relationship with her mother-in-law, affirmed Marge's suspicion—Edna had shared her dream disclosure. Obviously, the family suspected she was becoming senile and delusional. Marge decided to make no further mention of her nighttime trauma, but apparently, her decision of silence came to late. Despite her objections, Christy moved in.

Though the foreboding specter still prowled through her nights, Marge found solace in the fact her vow of silence seemed to be working. Her children became less protective, Christy even spoke of entering college mid-term . . . until two nights ago when the demonic dream resurfaced with a vengeance. Once again the man was descending the stairs; once again the car crept ominously closer to where Marge now stood at the crosswalk. She could just make out the figures of the three men inside, when a sudden mass of cold air swirled around her, immobilizing her. Unable to move, she could only scream out her frantic warning.

"Wake up, Grandma! Please, wake up!" Marge opened her eyes to discover Christy's face, contorted with fear and concern, hovering above her. While Marge insisted it had been no more than a leg cramp causing her to cry out, that same afternoon, Edna phoned begging Marge to make an appointment with a psychiatric counselor. Of course, Marge refused.

\*　　　\*　　　\*

From the lightness of the gray square on her bedroom wall, Marge guessed it to be around five o'clock. Hearing no sound from Christy's room, she released the air trapped in her lungs. Cautiously folding back the bedclothes, she slowly lowered her feet to the floor. Stripping the still damp nightgown over her head, she snuggled into the welcomed warmth of her chenille rob and slipped her feet into her fuzzy, well-worn bunny slippers, a long ago gift from Clifford she couldn't bring herself to throw away.

Stepping into the hall, she paused to listen at the door of the adjoining bedroom, then quietly crept down the stairway, clinging to the banister for the support her trembling knees denied her. In the kitchen, she lifted the carafe from the automatic coffeemaker but her suddenly-turned-spastic hands failed to direct the hot liquid into her waiting cup, splashing it, instead across the green marble countertop.

The horror of last night's nightmare, refusing to be left behind, had slithered down the steps behind her and now replayed its gruesome scenario. Once again, Marge was running toward the unaware victim, could clearly see the handsome, swarthy features, the dark hair springing crisply forward above black, bushy brows. Screams froze in her throat as the black car turned the corner and the long, slim object appeared through the open car window. From what now seemed but a few scant feet away, Marge watched as the tall man turned, saw his face suddenly distorted by surprise, then terror. Suddenly, the white marble steps turned red.

Sliding the carafe back onto its pedestal, Marge buried her face in shaking hands, her breath now coming in shuddering sobs. Was she losing her sanity? Had she lost the ability to determine reality from imagination? Perhaps Edna was right. Perhaps she should schedule an appointment with a counselor. But the dream was so vivid, so real. What did it mean? Did it bear a message? A chill shivered across her shoulders. If that were so, why was *she* having the dream?

A sudden thud startled her from the dark despair of her thoughts. Bewildered for only a moment, she realized it was the newspaper, delivered to her door every morning at this time. Dutifully, she stumbled across the room, opened the door and stooped to retrieve the periodical from her porch. Automatically, she unfolded the sheaf of printed pages.

Her breath deserted her in a small, barely audible gasp as her heart crashed against her rib cage. Knees turned liquid, she sank helplessly to the porch step. There, staring up at her from the front page was the familiar, dark swarthy face of the man in her dream, shot down, the headline said, on the steps of the U.S. Embassy.

An overwhelming sense of sorrow washed over her, mingled with an inexplicable feeling of guilt—guilt that somehow she could have, should have, prevented this tragedy. Involuntary tears found their way down her cheeks. Yet, bubbling beneath this confusing surge of emotion was the glimmer of hope. Perhaps now, her family would understand, would believe in her once again.

But most important, now the nightmares would finally stop—or would they?

# SINS OF THE FATHER

*Some weeks ago, an article appeared on the editorial page, an article written by a man of African descent. It was his contention that all Caucasians were guilty for the enslavement of his people. Even though they did not live in America at the time slavery was acceptable here, they were, he insisted, guilty merely by their European heritage.*

\*       \*       \*

A scowl drawing his bushy gray eyebrows together like two courting caterpillars, presiding Judge Bocelli peered over the top of his wire-rimmed glasses at the young man facing him across the courtroom desk.

"Mr. Anderson, do you fully understand the charges filed against you?"

With a barely perceptible lift of his broad shoulders, the sandy-haired young man, feet widespread, hands clasped behind him, fixed his steady gaze upon the judge. Dark, troubled eyes, startling in their contrast to his fair skin, were clouded with uncertainty. Yet, he spoke with confidence.

"I am aware of the charges, your Honor, but I'm not sure I fully understand them."

The gray caterpillars came together again above the judge's thin nose as he noisily cleared his throat. "Then, allow me to review them for you, Mr. Anderson. And I strongly urge you to pay close attention."

The judge adjusted his oval glasses as he lifted a sheaf of papers from the desk in front of him. He raised his eyes again to the young defendant. "You are Caucasian, are you not?"

A slight twitch appeared at the corner of the young man's mouth at the incongruity of the question. "Yes, Your Honor."

"And of European extraction?"

"That is correct, Your Honor."

Judge Bocelli glanced at the typewritten page before him. "By reason of heritage, Dr. Samuel Washington," the judge inclined his head toward a black man seated in the front row, "accuses you of having held his people in slavery, thereby condemning them to a legacy of poverty and, consequently, sub-standard living conditions. He demands full restitution from you for this injustice to his people."

The black man nodded his head vigorously, leaning to whisper to the man seated next to him. The judge glowered a reprimand, then selecting a second file from his desktop, took a moment to inspect its contents before returning his attention to the defendant.

"According to these records, your ancestors were among the first settlers moving westward in the late 1800's. Is that correct, Mr. Anderson?"

"It is, Your Honor."

The judge pursed his lips as he studied the paper in his hand. "By reason of heritage, Mr. Joseph Bluefeather deems you responsible for the death of his nation when his people were driven from their lands." Judge Bocelli glanced expectantly toward the red-skinned man, also seated in the front row. The man's face remained expressionless, a slight clenching of his jaw and narrowing of his eyes, the only sign of his affirmation.

Returning his attention to the page in front of him the judge continued. "Mr. Bluefeather demands restitution in the form of full payment for his father's lands, and further, insists special privileges be granted his people exempting them from restrictions of the white man's laws."

Judge Bocelli removed his glasses, wiping them carefully with a square of white linen he dug from his pocket. Balancing them once again on the narrow ridge of his nose, he opened the cover of a third file. "Your dossier, Mr. Anderson, indicates your parents were involved in a recent war with Japan. Do you deny this?"

The young man let his hands drop to his sides. "No, Your Honor, I do not."

Once again, Judge Bocelli cleared his throat. "Mr. Ito Yamamoto," he began. Seated at the far end of the front row, an ocher-skinned man dipped his head in acknowledgement. "By reason of heritage," the judge continued, "Mr. Yamamoto holds you accountable for the wrongful internment of his people, though American citizens, and the confiscation of their properties with no other cause than the circumstance of their birth. He demands justification for this unwarranted discrimination against his people." Carefully closing the file, Judge Bocelli folded his hands in front of him and once again peered over the rim of his glasses. "Do you deny any of these allegations, Mr. Anderson?"

The young man, who restricted his vision to the scuffed toes of his shoes during this dissertation, raised his eyes to meet the questioning gaze of the magistrate. "The facts are true, Your Honor."

The oaken chair squealed in protest as the judge adjusted his weight on its swivel base. "Then, Mr. Anderson, how do you plead to these charges? Guilty, or not guilty?"

The defendant squared his shoulders, his unflinching gaze never leaving the face of his interrogator. His reply bounced boldly from the walls of the tiny courtroom. "Not guilty, Your Honor."

There was a moment of silence, then a whirlpool of sound swirled about the room— first as whispers of surprise, then in voices of protest. Like a misplaced exclamation point, the crack of his gavel preceded the judge's anger. "Order! There will be order in this courtroom!" Like the rustling layers of a woman's petticoats, nervous whispers flitted about the room as silence gradually asserted itself. Judge Botcelli turned to the accused. "Now, Mr. Anderson, do you have a defense attorney or do you wish the court to appoint one to represent you?"

If the defendant was shaken by the reaction of his peers, his voice, still strong and confident, did not betray him. "I do not wish representation,

Your Honor. I have no witnesses to call in my defense. I ask only that you allow me to make an argument in my own behalf."

Once again, the judge's gray eyebrows courted one another. "This is highly irregular." He hesitated, studying the face patiently awaiting his reply. Apparently satisfied with what he found there, "Very well," he relented. "You may proceed."

For the first time, the fair-skinned, sandy-haired young man turned to face his accusers. Slowly, his dark, gentle eyes traveled across the three hostile faces confronting him. When finally he spoke, his voice carried no trace of recrimination.

"You have accused me, by reason of heredity, of many heinous crimes committed against my fellow man, " he began. "I don't deny the gravity of these acts. But, before you condemn me by reason of my ancestry, I ask you to remember, these same ancestors also suffered at the hands of others, were forced to seek haven in this country to escape, among other things, debtors' prison, and religious persecution.

The accused turned to face the black man. "Dr. Washington, you claim it is I who enslaved your people. Let me point out, your bible reveals slavery has always been with us. Can you deny that your own people were involved in slave trading? Yet, without doubt, it was a shameful time in this country's history. Let me remind you, however, it was a man of my heritage who tried to set things right." The young man closed his eyes and when he reopened them, they had grown darker with sadness. "Dr. Washington, I cannot afford to, nor do I wish to, send your people back to their Africa where even now they struggle against the yoke of apartheid. I ask, instead, you consider the opportunities available to you, opportunities that have enabled you to affix the honorable title of 'Doctor' before your name."

Clasping his hands behind his back, the defendant moved to the second of his accusers. "Mr. Bluefeather." He waited until steely eyes met his. "You would hold me accountable for the destruction of your once proud people, of driving them from their homes. Yet, is it not true, before my ancestors arrived in this country, your own tribes warred among themselves, driving one another from lands they wished to possess? Still, ours was a heartless injustice, one I cannot reverse. I can only hope you will take advantage of opportunities available to you; that one day you no longer wish to set yourselves apart, but will bury the past with your dead."

Slowly, the young man approached the third, and last plaintiff, seated at the end of the row. "Mr. Yamamoto." He spoke softly, his voice barely audible. "It is your charge which is most painful. It recalls a tragic, most disgraceful time in our history, a memory which will not fade quickly." A sigh escaped his lips. "It was a time of hysteria. In the name of self-preservation, a hasty and ill-advised decision was made to condemn your people by reason of heritage . . . as you now wish to condemn me."

The defendant moved back to the center of the room, still facing his accusers. "I ask you, each of you, to forgive my father, and my father's father, and his father before him. But, more important, I ask you to remember, I am not my father. I am an American, just as you are. Regardless of how we came to be here, we are all now a part of this country, a country founded on the premise of "We the People." There have been many mistakes in our past, but with each generation, things do get better. If we are to continue moving forward, we must discard such labels as 'us' and 'them' and cast off the crippling chains of self-pity. There is a lot still not right with this country, but only 'we' can change that."

The defendant turned to face the judge, his dark eyes now snapping with defiance. "Your Honor, it is my belief no man should be held responsible for the deeds of another, or for the sins of his father. For that reason, I plead 'not guilty' to these charges."

No sound disturbed the uneasy silence that followed. Scanning the expectant faces filling the courtroom, Judge Bocelli's fingers tightened about the shaft of the judicial gavel. Without a doubt, he knew the decision he was about to make would prove to be the toughest of his career.

If the decision were yours, how would you rule?

# THE CONTRACT

"Never lose eye contact with your customer."

If you asked for one thing standing out in the memory of my Mixology training, it would be a surprising scrap of trivia revealing that neither a crook or a drunk can look you in the eye when he's talking to you. I hadn't forgotten that priceless bit of advice, it had just temporarily submerged itself in the quicksand of sludge filling my brain . . . a sludge that builds up after too many nights behind the bar, listening to the woeful outpourings of an endless stream of misfits and losers. After awhile, you learn to tune them out. I guess that's when I got careless.

+ + +

Fishing yesterday's balled-up sock from inside my left shoe, I dragged it over my foot and reached for its mate. My searching fingers met nothing but the inside smoothness of my right shoe. *Damn!* I was in no mood this morning to crawl around under the bed looking for dirty footwear. I yanked the lone sock from my foot and flung it impatiently across the room. Leaning across the end of the bed, I snatched a clean, rolled-up pair of socks from the suitcase resting on the luggage rack.

*I wish I could get that damned drunk off my mind. Too bad my foresight wasn't as good as my hindsight.* For the hundredth time, I mentally kicked myself for serving him that last pitcher of beer. No telling how many beers the guy had at how many other bars before he hit mine. What really bugged me was he'd fooled me so completely, taken me in like I was some rube just off the turnip truck. It wasn't until he pulled that knife, I realized how crazy drunk he was.

"Honey, have you called down to the front desk yet?" Sandy's muffled voice came from behind the bathroom door.

I stifled the sigh of irritation forming in my chest; forcing it to slip slowly, quietly between my lips. My wife's hearing was almost as acute as her sense of smell. I'd been awake half the night, listening to her complain about the odor in our room.

"They're probably cooking tomorrow's chow," I'd suggested, hoping to pacify her.

"But we're on the fifth floor," she persisted. "We shouldn't be able to get kitchen odors all the way up here."

"It probably comes up through the vents. I'll call the desk in the morning," I promised. I didn't figure it was important enough to lose a night's sleep over. Hotel rooms always smell funny to me. Besides, it was just Sandy being Sandy. She was a great housekeeper, but away from home, she complained about everything; the silverware was dirty, the tablecloth was soiled, the glasses were spotted . . . the room smelled.

"We can stop at the desk on our way out to breakfast," I shouted back at her through the closed door.

I'd told Sandy about the episode with the drunk, how, while he held a roomful of shocked customers mesmerized with his weapon, I managed to slip into the backroom and call the police.

What I didn't tell her was the threat the guy made when the police took him away.

I felt the same cold chill wash over me as I recalled the smoldering hatred in those dark, bloodshot eyes as he glared back over his shoulder. "You'll get yours," he snarled. Somehow, it didn't sound like the ranting of a drunk.

Another thing I didn't tell Sandy was that Officer Donovan was waiting at the tavern when I opened the next morning. "Thought you might want to know what happed to your 'friend' last night," he offered. "You ever heard of the Brotherhood?"

I had. Operating under the guise of a loan company, rumors connected them with underworld drug trafficking. Not somebody you'd want to tangle with. I raised my eyebrows in question, pretty certain I didn't want to hear the answer.

Donovan nodded. "A member in good standing. Calls himself 'Mac, the Knife'. In case you're interested," he added. "He's already out on bail."

"But what else could I do?" I was feeling a little sick to my stomach. "He pulled a knife. Why would they . . .?" I swallowed the rest of the words along with the bile rising in my throat and groped beneath the counter for my anti-acids.

"Go figure," Donovan shrugged. "Anyway, you might want to make yourself scarce for awhile, take the Missus on a vacation for a few days, just until this cools down."

I didn't waste any time. I called our travel agent, told her to set us up in a nice hotel in Reno for a few days. Then I called Sandy. It hadn't been easy convincing her I was really serious about closing the business and taking off on a vacation. She finally agreed to the trip, but only if we stopped to visit her Aunt Ada on the way. I'd have agreed to raising Saint Bernards about then, if it would get us out of town. I made a mental note to call the hotel and change our arrival date.

*         *         *

The bathroom door opened and Sandy stepped out. I paused to let my eyes enjoy the feast. Even after twenty-two years of marriage, she was still a pretty great looking gal. She'd brushed her reddish-blonde hair back in that style I liked so well, while the green sweater she wore brought out the subtle green of her eyes. So, maybe she did have a few quirks that weren't easy to live with. I knew life would be pretty empty without her. A restless moth of uneasiness gave birth in my stomach as a chilling thought occurred to me; what if that creep, "Mac whatever", followed us here? For the first time, I wondered if maybe I had put Sandy in danger as well as myself.

"Come on, Handsome." Sandy was smiling at me. "Let's go break the bank."

Forget what they say about only being lucky *either* in love *or* cards. Today, I was both. After stopping at the hotel desk to suggest they close off the kitchen vents to keep the odors out of our room, we hit the casinos. Man you name it; slots, blackjack, poker, I just couldn't lose. We were riding the crest of gambler's delirium when we finally returned to our hotel. My hand on her elbow, I guided Sandy toward the open elevator doors, thinking to myself how beautiful she looked, her face flushed, her eyes sparkling with excitement. Until he touched my arm, I hadn't noticed the desk clerk approaching us.

"Excuse me, Sir," the uniformed young man whispered in my ear. "Would you please come with me?"

That uneasy feeling was stirring again in my stomach. I reached automatically for the Rollaids tucked in my pocket. "What is it?" I demanded. "What's wrong?"

"Please, Sir, if you would just follow me." His nervousness was becoming contagious. "The manager wishes to speak with you."

"What's the matter?" Sandy hissed into my ear.

I ushered her to an ornate brocaded settee positioned near the desk. "Wait here," I instructed. "I'll find out what's going on."

As I entered the door to his office, a nattily dressed little man rose hastily from the chair behind his desk. His hand outstretched, he moved quickly toward me, his lips pulled into a smile which had not yet been transmitted to his eyes. "Mr. Andrews," he gushed. "We thank you for coming by. We do apologize for the inconvenience, but we found it necessary to move you into another room."

"Another room?" I parroted.

"Actually, we've moved you into the Penthouse. We do apologize for the inconvenience and we do hope you . . ."

"Is there a problem?" I interrupted.

The eyes of the 'man in charge' shifted to some vague spot over my shoulder, then moved to conduct an intensive study of the carpet at my feet. I was fairly certain he wasn't drunk and hoped it safe to assume he wasn't a crook, so I knew there was something terribly wrong.

I repeated. "What's the problem?"

"Well . . .ah . . . you see . . .." Closing his eyes, he dragged a hand through his thinning hair, then released a ragged sigh. "Mr. Andrews," he began. "I believe it might be necessary for us to rely upon your discretion in what is a . . . a very delicate matter." I watched his jaw muscle flexing as he wrestled with his decision. "I'm afraid there has been a most unfortunate accident."

"An accident?" My brain cells no longer seemed to be functioning.

"Yes, well," the distraught little man struggled on. "You see, when you changed your reservation two days ago, we booked another gentlemen, temporarily, of course, into your room. "We . . . ah . . . we thought he had checked out, but . . . "

"But what?" The prickly hairs on the back of my neck were now standing at full attention.

"The maids, checking out your complaint this morning, you know, about the odor?" The poor man's eyes were now roving wildly about the room. "Well, they discovered . . . under the bed . . ."

From what seemed light years away, I watched the hotel manager's pale lips move, heard the far-off hollowness of his voice.

"His throat . . . it seems his throat had been cut."

# ARMAGEDDON

Like an over-ripe tomato, the round autumn moon hovers above the horizon, its once yellow brilliance now tinged an angry red by the smoke and dust hanging heavy in the night air.

A violent spasm of coughing convulses my throat as my lungs reject the acrid air I've drawn into them. Through watering eyes, I gaze at the landscape of destruction surrounding me. The once stately Tudor that had been my home now cringes at my feet, a mass of crumbled brick and tile, while the crushed blue metal of my shiny new Mercedes lies pinned mercilessly to the earth by the huge maple once shading the flagstone walkway. The gazebo tilts crazily on its side, still wrapped in the possessive embrace of the bougainvillea.

I reach to brush the stinging moisture from my eyes and can only stare stupidly at the blood suddenly covering my hand. What happened? Hysterically, my confused brain rattles the closed doors of my memory, struggling to find the key to reality. What happened? Then, I remember.

There is noise . . . a lot of noise. The ballgame . . . Andy and I . . . . watching the Mariners . . . the fourth inning . . . the Kingdome, exploding with the roar of excited fans. I turn to say something to Andy, when suddenly the rumbling roar seems to burst from the screen, into the living room, rattling the windows, sending lamps into wild, unrehearsed jigs upon glass-topped end tables.

"Earthquake!" a shrill voice . . . mine or Andy's? . . . shrieks. "Earthquake!" Andy's voice, shouting, "Outside! Get outside!"

Grandmother's heirloom vase, teetering on the edge of the mantle. I stagger across the heaving floor, reach to catch vase . . . .

Dazed, I stare around me at the unfamiliar desolation. Andy, where is Andy? The sound of voices penetrates my stupor and I become aware there are others out there, like myself. Anxiously, I scramble from my prison of rubble and stumble out onto the roadway, now a pile of jagged rock and concrete. Carefully, I pick my way along the hazardous maze of debris which, just a few hours before, had been the street outside our home. Peering into the semi-darkness, I can make out a cluster of shadowy forms, huddled together, their muted voices betraying their fear. I recognize some of my neighbors; there's George, but I don't see Alice. I see Carol . . . and Bill. But, where is Andy?

As I draw nearer the circle, I see a man standing in its midst, a tall stranger I've never seen before. Even in the defused light of the pale moon, I see how handsome he is . . . no, not handsome, beautiful, with thick, black wavy hair, a strong square jaw and teeth that gleam in his bronze face when he smiles. I cannot explain the chill shuddering through me as I notice his eyes . . .dark, piercing, so cold. Yet, his voice, while forceful, demanding, is soft and strangely comforting.

I edge closer to hear what he is saying. "We must leave this place, now, quickly." It is a command with no option of refusal.

But, of course, he is right. What if there is another quake? He cautions us to stay with him if we wish to reach safety, then turns and strides away. Eagerly, we crowd to follow closely behind him. As we move down the street, other figures join us, some I recognize, others are strangers. All are eager to be free of this nightmare. I do not see Andy.

I don't know how many hours we have been walking. The sky in the east is growing light but the cool air of the night still travels with us. We are in a valley now, its shadowy sides rising steeply on either side. No one has spoken during our journey, not even our leader, though now and then, he turns to flash us an encouraging smile. Yet, I see no warmth in his smile, or in those disturbingly cold eyes. A vague uncertainty plucks at the edge of my sub-conscious, an uncertainty I see reflected in the face of the traveler beside me. Despite our weariness and doubts, we continue on.

Suddenly, I hear the sound, or rather I feel it, vibrating through the soles of my shoes; a rumbling, thunder-like sound roiling just beneath the surface of the ground. The others have heard it too, for they've stopped walking, as have I. As one, our gaze is drawn to the top of the valley. There, we see them, like magnificent Olympic gods, cloaked in garments of white— mounted on great white horses, they poise at the crest of the hill.

Awe-struck, we stare at them while an uneasy chill of foreboding prickles up my spine, lifting the hairs at the nape of my neck. In the next moment, they are swooping down upon us, brandishing their terrible swords, the hooves of their powerful steed jarring the earth.

I am running. Around me, I hear terrified screams of panic. *I must escape!* Someone, running beside me, stumbles, falls, cries out for help, but I do not stop. *I must escape!* I hear the pounding hoof beats behind me drawing closer. My lungs have become organs of pain, laboring to fill my ruthless demands. My imprisoned heart pounds frantically at the wall of my chest.

I feel the beast's hot breath scalding my shoulders. *I cannot escape!* A cold fungus of despair spreads through me, devouring my last remnant of strength. I know I cannot escape!

He is beside me, now. I see the flared nostrils of the great stallion, his wild glittering eyes; the horseman astride him towers over me. As the white-clad angel raises his sword above his head, a shaft of sunlight glints upon the glittering metal, illuminating the avenger's face.

I cannot move. I cannot breathe. I can only stare with horror into those familiar, beloved features.

"Andy!" The scream tears itself from my lips as his terrible sword plunges into my chest.

# TODAY'S FORECAST
# MOSTLY SUNNY

# THE DAYS OF AUTUMN

Every ear of corn growing there bore a likeness to a woman weeping, as, head bowed, long silken tresses hiding her sorrow, she mourned the passing of youth and the loss of the loves once hers when first she blossomed, then grew to maturity.

Soon they would be gone from her forever: the sun with its warm, passionate embrace: the soft, fleeting caresses of the summer wind: the moist, gentle kisses of the evening rain.

Her body now ripe and heavy, she clung vainly to the aging, withering stalks once nurturing her; their bright green leaves once swaying and dancing in the spring breeze, now rattle, brittle, in the restless autumn air.

And the days dwindled down . . . soon it would be harvest time.

# AN ACT OF KINDNESS

I had no idea how long I'd been lying there on the cold concrete, absorbing the bone-chilling dampness now trapped inside my body by my soggy, mud-splattered coat. Pain had diluted the keen edges of time while time, in turn, had diffused the sharp shards of pain so recently slashing through my side. Though I now felt only a dull steady ache, I was still careful to make no sudden moves lest I re-awaken the red waves of agony and nausea lurking but a twitch of a muscle away.

Moving only my eyes, I probed the darkness of my surroundings. In the dim light from a street lamp, I could make out the dingy gray wall of brick across the alley from me. Instantly, I recognized the grafitti-covered surface of the Pine Street Tavern. At least, I knew where I was. This was my territory. I knew every last alley, doorway and garbage can lining First Avenue from Pike Street to Jackson. I'd been panhandling these streets for eight years, knew every crevice, every crack in the sidewalk; knew the best places for an easy touch and the ones wisest to avoid. How, then, did I end up lying in this dark alleyway with my side ripped open?

Slowly, reluctantly, tortured recollections shuddered free from my pain-numbed brain. I had been in Pike Place Market, rated A-1 for panhandlers. I was working the fish market today, always a good place for a handout with the all that fish-throwing keeping tourists in a partying mood. I was moving in on what looked like a soft touch when, suddenly, I heard someone yell. I looked up in time to see a huge fish gaff sailing through the air, headed straight for me. I jumped out of the way, thought I managed to dodge it, until I felt the searing pain in my side, felt my skin ripping apart. I ran.

I closed my eyes, willing those agonizing memories back into the confining prison of my sub-conscious. What would happen to me now, I wondered? No one keeps track of the homeless. Would I lie here until I slowly bled to death? No, not like this! I opened my mouth to cry out but the plea scratching its way up my throat and past my lips was scarcely more than a pathetic whimper. In desperation, I again opened my mouth to cry for help when a familiar sound reached me years . . . the clickity-clack of Old Bertha's grocery cart, the unmistakable scuff of her footsteps as she shuffled along behind it.

Old Bertha has worked this neighborhood for nearly as long as I. A ratty wool cap pulled low over dank, colorless hair, she wore a ragged gray overcoat covering no one knew how many equally ragged garments beneath. Her feet encased in oversized boots, Bertha could be seen shuffling along the waterfront streets of Seattle almost anytime, day or night, pushing a cast-away grocery cart with its one flat wheel and all her worldly goods, ahead of her. I never bothered her . . . she never bothered me. Now, she paused and I could see her peering curiously into my tunnel of darkness. I wondered if she would see me. After all, I am black.

A shiver of relief ran down my spine as, dragging her cart alongside her, Bertha moved into the alley. Her wrinkled face hovered close to mine as she bent over me.

"Well, if you don't look like somethin' the cat dragged in." I cringed as, straightening, she threw back her head and filled the alley with the caustic cackle of her laughter.

Still chuckling to herself, Bertha plunged a hand into her basket of unknown treasures. "Don't worry, Honey," she rasped. "Old Bertha'll fix you up."

With a cylinder of unknown contents in her hand, she once again leaned over me. "Needs salt," I heard her mutter before the red waves of pain and nausea once again invaded my body. I could hear my own screams bouncing off the outside wall of the Pine Street Tavern. I lashed out at her, but with my head pinned firmly to the hard concrete by her surprisingly strong arm, none of the blows from my flailing limbs made contact. Gradually, the stinging misery subsided and I grew calm. I was aware of little else now but the throbbing in my side.

Through the blurred vision of my watering eyes, I saw Bertha remove her fingerless gloves exposing her reddened, chapped hands. "Everything's gonna be better, now," she crooned softly, running her gnarled fingers through my coarse hair. "You'll see." Her raw hands felt like silk to me.

Slipping one hand beneath my head and the other beneath my hip, Bertha lifted me carefully from the cold concrete. With gentleness betraying the woman within, she lowered me onto the pile of rags filling her cart. "Don't you worry none, old cat," she croaked. "Old Bertha's gonna take care of you."

I felt a purr beginning to rumble at the back of my throat. Gratefully, I closed my eyes and let sleep and Old Bertha take over.

# FROM SISSY, WITH LOVE

On soft, fog-shrouded feet, the cold winter dampness crept stealthily from Puget Sound, poking icy fingers inside upturned collars, probing relentlessly beneath tightly buttoned jackets. Moisture dripped with monotonous regularity from right-angled street signs, clouding the impassive faces of metal meters standing guard over nearly empty streets. A green neon tree spread its gaseous branches above the doorway of the Pine Street Tavern, its reflection shimmering on the glistening pavement

Three teen-aged boys lounged against the building's whitewashed brick, now chipped and defaced with angry graffiti. An occasional wisp of gray smoke rose into the air as each youth, pinching it between his fingers, inhaled the sweetness of a tightly rolled joint before passing it on to his companions.

Shoulders hunched against the chill, a tattered wool cap pulled low over his forehead, a solitary pedestrian shuffled down the rain-washed sidewalk. Cold-reddened fingers of one hand held together the narrow collar of his thin jacket, while the other clutched the brown bag protruding from his sagging pocket. Momentarily caught in the illuminating headlights of a taxicab, he hesitated, staring like a startled deer into the blinding glare. Then, fingers tightening about the brown bag, he darted into the welcoming darkness of an alleyway.

A few blocks away at Third and Broadway, a silver and gray bus sloshed to a halt alongside the curb. Its doors opened, regurgitated a

171

young man in the olive drab of an army uniform, then whooshed shut again as, shifting gears growling in protest, the Greyhound rumbled back into traffic.

The young soldier hesitated, taking a moment to establish his bearings in the maelstrom of activity suddenly engulfing him. From every direction, holiday lights splashed garish reflections of red and green onto the glistening pavement, turning sidewalks into a distorted image of a Christmas watercolor. An aggregation of automobiles shouldered their way down the street like a row of linebackers, each vying for the best position, while restless adversaries hovered at a stoplight, eager to enter the competition. From a department store window across the avenue, an animated larger-than-life Santa waved with cheerful monotony to the throngs of grim-faced last-minute shoppers.

The young soldier turned away from the mayhem of street traffic only to find himself directly in the path of an agitated woman shopper, her scowling face a contradiction to the gaily-wrapped packages filling her arms. Impatiently, she jostled against him, forcing the serviceman from the curbing and into the gutter.

His hand darted quickly to where a wallet formed a square bulge in his hip pocket. His fingers traced the comforting reassurance of its bulk, easing the consternation tightening his youthful features. More important to him than the month's pay it contained was the picture it sheltered: its inscription "To my dear brother Alex, From Sissy, With Love," scrawled across it in a twelve-year-old's handwriting. The crafted artifact of Moroccan leather was a gift from his little sister the last Christmas they'd spent together—the Christmas before the accident. Alex swallowed against the surge of grief welling into his throat as a cruel memory replayed the nightmarish tragedy: His father behind the wheel of the speedboat, turning to wave at a laughing Sissy following him on water skies. He swerved in time to miss the unseen dock, but not in time for Sissy. Her frail young body crashed into the floating structure, splintering its wood; splintering their family.

Vowing never to return to that seething cauldron of grief, guilt and angry recriminations, sixteen-year-old Alex, with the aid of an altered birth certificate, found escape in an early military enlistment. It seemed a solution, gave him a place to sleep, three meals a day, constant, if questionable, companionship. But he hadn't anticipated the loneliness of the holiday, his first Christmas away from everything familiar. Facing the prospect of spending Christmas Eve at the base, and with no place else to go, he'd opted for the holiday excitement of the big city. At this moment, with cold water seeping into his government-issue shoes, saturating his G. I. socks, he wasn't so sure his choice was the right one.

Reclaiming his position upon the curb, Alex glanced into the faces of the self-absorbed mass of humanity scurrying past him, but saw no friendliness there. He realized, too late, this wasn't where he would find the Yuletide spirit. A quiet bar, his young rationale decided, maybe a good drunk, was how he'd spend his holiday. Turning his back on the commercial bustle, Alex flipped up the collar of his Army-issue jacket and headed toward the waterfront.

*       *       *

Overhead, the green and white sign identified the corner as the junction of Second Avenue and Pine Street. Shivering as cold air from the waterfront invaded the inadequate shelter of his Eisenhower jacket, Alex studied his surroundings—decidedly bleaker than the frantic commercial bedlam he'd just left. Halfway down the block, a "Welcome" sign flickered above the Second Avenue Mission. A few doors nearer, a pathetic little plastic tree adorned the window of a pawnshop, faded ornaments clinging tenaciously to its drooping branches.

As he watched, a middle-aged, too-plump woman detached herself from the doorway and sauntered toward him. Her shabby coat, trimmed with matted, nondescript fur, hung loosely open. The too-bright lipstick and excessive rouge contradicted the youthful efforts of her too-short skirt and low-cut blouse. She paused beside him, an inviting smile curving her lips. Alex turned away from the overwhelming fragrance of gardenia eddying about her. Sensing his silent rejection to her unspoken invitation, she shrugged her indifference and ambled back down the sidewalk on her aimless quest for companionship.

On the opposite street corner, a shivering Salvation Army volunteer hunched over the red, tripod-supported pot in front of him, the tinny sound of his bell declaring to an apathetic audience, his loyalty and dedication to his chosen cause.

Alex's wandering gaze suddenly fastened itself upon the culmination of his search. At the foot of the darkened street leading to First Avenue, a flickering green light hovered above the doorway of the Pine Street Tavern, his just-elected destination.

Overhead, the signal light turned green, sending Alex hurrying to the opposite curb. His arrival launched the hopeful bell-ringer into an increased frenzy of activity. Alex started to brush past him, then hesitated, remembering the month's pay in his wallet. "What the heck," he thought, digging into his pocket, "it's Christmas." A wave of memories crowded into a painful lump at the back of his throat as he stared into the face of the young girl smiling at him from inside the square of soft leather. It was a moment before Alex was aware of the bell-ringer staring at him, questioning eyes bright with anticipation. Yanking out a twenty-dollar bill, Alex crammed it into the pot swinging from its tripod and turned toward the bleak promise beckoning from beneath the neon pine tree.

He passed the darkened alleyway, barely glancing at three teen-aged smokers lounging outside the tavern, when he sensed a sudden movement behind him. It was possible he had no warning of danger until he felt an explosion of pain behind his ear. Yet, perhaps he did feel the crunch as his knees struck the hard pavement, its wet chill soaking into the thin fabric of his uniform. He was only vaguely aware of rough hands tugging and ripping at his pockets, bright lights stabbing his eyes, retreating footsteps slapping against wet concrete and then . . . dark oblivion.

*       *       *

With swiftness born of practice, the three young teenagers surrounded their victim. Once the soldier crumpled to the sidewalk, the older boy knelt beside the still body. Hastily riffling through the uniform, he pulled a package of cigarettes from a pocket, stuffing it into his own denim one.

"Hurry it up, you guys," he hissed at his two younger companions. "Get his watch."

He plunged a hand into the soldier's hip pocket and the corners of his mouth lifted in a wicked grin as his fingers closed about the familiar shape of a wallet. He hesitated, slowly rubbing his thumb over the mesmeric softness of the four by four square of leather. In the next instant, he was being blinded as a taxicab rounded the corner, capturing them in the brilliance of its headlights. An expletive tore itself from the teen's lips. Scooping the green bills from their warm nest, he crammed them into his pocket and flung the incriminating wallet away from him. He heard it splat against the brick wall of the tavern as he hurled himself after his companions already sprinting down the alley, while the smiling face of a young girl was left to stare into the night's dark mist.

*       *       *

Cowering in the dank alleyway, Ernie wrapped his arms tightly about himself in a vain attempt to stem the uncontrollable shivering of his body, the terrible chattering of his teeth. Crouching behind a garbage can, he witnessed the mugging in front of the tavern. Cringing in terror when the muggers' flight carried them too near his place of refuge, he quickly flattened his body against the brick wall, heedless to the consequences of his action. Fear kept him immobilized until he felt the growing dampness at his side. His hand darted to his pocket. Pulling forth the soggy bag, he watched with watery, red-rimmed eyes as the life of his liquid lover dripped through the thin brown paper, splattering onto the alley's concrete floor.

Letting the sack of shattered glass slip from his fingers, Ernie stumbled into the street. He paid no attention to the seemingly lifeless form stretched out upon the sidewalk. His attention turned, instead, to the brown square of leather lying a few feet away. Steadying himself against the building with one hand for a moment, Ernie stooped to snatch the wallet from the gutter. With numb fingers, he clawed hopefully into its depths, but the muggers had been thorough. Except for an ID card and a photograph, the wallet was empty. Disappointment filling his rheumy eyes, Ernie stared dully at the happy child smiling up at him

A soft moan rose from the inert figure lying on the pavement, jolting Ernie from his stupor. His eyes darted nervously down the dimly lit avenue to where a taxicab paused at the corner of First and Pine, a blinking turn signal announcing its imminent arrival at the scene of the mugging. Fear twisting his slack features, Ernie lurched across the street, scarcely aware he still clutched the sodden wallet in his fist.

His stumbling, erratic steps carried him around the corner and onto Second Avenue where, sagging against the rough stone edifice of the Army/Navy Surplus store, he hungrily filled his lungs with ragged gulps of air. Only then was he aware the square of tanned hide still clenched in his hand. Once again, his chest tightened with fear. His brain, though dulled by an unlimited infusion of cheap wine, could still reason that, with the evidence in his possession, there was no doubt but that he would be accused of mugging that unlucky soldier.

*Who would believe him, a homeless wino?* He knew, somehow, he had to get rid of the wallet. His frantic gaze searched the sidewalk for a garbage can, a trash receptacle, anyplace where he could rid himself of this brown albatross. His eyes darted across the street to where a Salvation Army volunteer tended a little red pot dangling from a black tripod, his tiny brass bell heralding a cause for the needy. Ernie staggered from the curb, was halfway across the intersection, when he hesitated, rubbing his thumb over the leather, caressing its softness. He hadn't drifted so far from his past life that he no longer recognized quality. The wallet might be worth something, an inner voice suggested, maybe even a bottle of Thunderbird wine.

His staggering momentum carried Ernie to the opposite curb. The Collector of Pennies for the Poor halted the insistent plea of the tinkling brass bell and peered at Ernie, eyes narrowed in suspicion. Wavering uncertainly, Ernie lifted his chin, squaring his shoulders in an attempt at defiance. Fumbling into the wallet, his groping fingers closed around the card of identification. With a haughty flourish of mock disdain, he crammed the rectangle of cardboard into the little red pot before turning on his heel, his unsteady gait carrying him back across the intersection, the brown leather wallet still gripped in his hand.

It wasn't until he reached the opposite corner of Second and Pine he dared glance at his treasure and the promise it held. Oh, how he longed for oblivion in the arms of his liquid mistress. Goaded by the urgency of his need, his impatient gaze razed both sides of the street, resting for a moment on the pawnshop. No, no, too risky, he decided. They knew him too well, would think he had stolen property and call the police. How then, he agonized, was he going to make use of his find?

A cruel, toxemic brain paraded the tantalizing rows of Thunderbird and MD20 wine bottles lining the shelves of the Pike Street Deli. *That's it*! He almost shouted aloud with the joy of discovery. The all-night delicatessen where he cashed his "rehab" checks . . . bought his wine. Surely the wallet would be worth something to someone at the deli, he reasoned . . . maybe even earn him a euphoria-inducing bottle of Thunderbird.

Shivering, Ernie drew his thin coat more closely about him, his steps quickening with anticipation. His eager stride faltered when, belatedly, he realized his route would take him past the Mission, a place filled with people who would divorce him from his liquid love; people who sought to conquer him with his own guilt. It was a place he avoided until, at month's end, with his rehab funds depleted, cold weather and hunger drove him into their waiting arms. But he wanted nothing to do with them this night. With courage born of desire and nurtured by anticipation, Ernie moved cautiously to the edge of the sidewalk. If he could just ease by unnoticed . . ..

Perhaps it was the combination of too little food, too much wine, rendering him helpless against tantalizing odors, snaking beneath the closed doors of the Mission to mercilessly assail him. Dizziness filled his head as Ernie felt his foot slip on the curbing. Suddenly, he was lying in the gutter, aware of cold water soaking through his threadbare jacket. Concerned faces hovered above his; helping hands were lifting him, guiding him across the pavement.

A rush of warm air enveloped him, surrounded him with the yeasty smell of freshly baked bread, the mouth-watering aroma of roasted fowl. Across the room, an anemic shroud of tiny lights adorning its branches, a little Christmas tree bravely attempted to brighten the room. From somewhere in the foggy recesses of Ernie's mind, a small uneasy voice whispered, *The wallet, get rid of the wallet.*

Friendly voices, helping hands tugging at his wet jacket, urging him forward, past the Mission Box, placed by the door to receive contributions of clothing for the needy. Reaching out as if to steady himself, Ernie grabbed the edge of the receptacle— let the wallet slip from his hand. Then, with a helpless sigh of resignation, he surrendered to an irresistible euphoria of belonging.

*             *             *

His hands gripping the steering wheel, Harvey cautiously guided his aging taxicab along the wet, glistening pavement of the dimly lit street. Usually he could pick up a return fare when he delivered a customer to a posh hotel, but there wasn't much chance he'd pick up a fare tonight, here on First Avenue, not one he'd want at his back anyway. The waterfront wasn't his regular beat; he usually worked the uptown area. But evidently there was a big reception going on at the Edgewater

Inn where he'd just made his last drop. What a way to spend Christmas Eve, he thought. He was glad he had a job that kept him busy. If it wasn't for that . . . and Edith, he'd probably be spending the evening in some bar himself.

Droplets of water splashed against the windshield, heralding the return of a persistent rain dousing the city earlier that afternoon. Lowering one hand from the steering wheel, Harvey set the wipers into motion. He probably shouldn't be critical about how others spent the holidays, he thought. He and Edith didn't make much of Christmas anymore. It just . . . it just wasn't the same without Jimmy. That familiar ache knotted itself in his chest at the thought of their only son, Jimmy.

\*　　　\*　　　\*

It was Harvey's idea, but Edith agreed, to move to the West Coast so the could be close to Jimmy while he was stationed at Fort Lewis, a military base just outside Seattle. They should have gone back to North Dakota when Jimmy shipped out. Instead, they decided to stay on. Harvey went to work driving a taxi; Edith took a night job cleaning business offices. They wanted to be here when their son came back.

But he didn't come back.

\*　　　\*　　　\*

Harvey blinked away the moisture stinging his eyelids. He knew that's when they should have gone back home, back to their little Mom and Pop grocery store in North Dakota. But he couldn't face the memories waiting there: Jimmy growing up, Jimmy starring on the football team, Christmas Eves with Jimmy. Instead, they stayed here, in Seattle, far away from anything reminding them of their son. For Harvey, each day was spent hoping, praying, while peering into the face of every soldier on the street. After all, the telegram said "missing in action," not killed, only "missing." He couldn't leave, not until he was sure.

Harvey glanced at his watch. Most of the offices were closing early this evening but, still, it would probably be another couple of hours before Edith finished her cleaning job. Maybe he'd head back uptown, there were always a few late shoppers in a hurry to get home. He turned his cab onto Pine Street.

Suddenly caught in the brightness of the cab's headlights, three teenaged boys, crouching over a shapeless bundle on the sidewalk, turned startled faces toward him, then sprang to their feet. "Hoodlums" muttered Harvey, as, glancing in the rear view mirror, he saw them dart into the darkened alleyway. "Up to no good." For some reason, uneasiness, an unexplainable gut feeling, knotted itself in his stomach. Instead of continuing up Pine Street, Harvey made a right turn onto Second Avenue, another on Pike, until he was once again navigating the dimness of First Avenue.

Harvey eased the cab to a stop at the intersection of First and Pine. Waiting for the light to turn green, he watched the wipers angrily flinging droplets of rain from the windshield. Their agitated flip-flop only aggravated his own, sudden impatience—impatience with the weather, with the season, with himself. He was being foolish, wasting time being concerned over the antics of some hoodlum teenagers; even more foolish, he admitted, hoping to find his lost son on the streets of Seattle, to say nothing of his thoughtless expectation that Edith put up with his fantasies. He knew it was difficult for her, too. Christmas was the worst, when, he knew, for his sake, she tried to treat it as if it was no special day. A weary sigh escaped his lips. Tomorrow, maybe he'd take Edith someplace nice for dinner.

The light turned green. Harvey eased his foot onto the gas pedal and turned onto Pine Street. Instinctively, he slammed on the brakes as the headlights illuminated the frightened features of a skid-row wino, and Harvey saw the still form lying on the sidewalk. Giving little forethought to his reaction, Harvey swerved into an illegal park against the curb, and jumped from behind the steering wheel. But the street person was already disappearing around the corner of the Army/Navy Surplus building, the haste of his staggering gait abetted by fear.

Quickly, Harvey knelt beside the inert figure on the sidewalk, his anxious glance taking in the brown olive drab of the soldier's uniform . . . the red liquid oozing from the bluish welt raising above the victim's ear. For a moment, the terrible re-occurring nightmare plaguing Harvey's sleep washed over him, and, as in his dream, the form he knelt over was that of his son.

"Jimmy!" The anguished cry tore itself from his soul as Harvey cradled the unconscious stranger in his arms. "Jimmy!"

The young man stirred, groaning softly as he tried to lift his head. The sound invaded Harvey's private purgatory, brutally jerking him back to reality . . . the soldier in his arms was not his son. Carefully, his hands beneath the soldier's arms, Harvey lifted the young man to his feet, steadying him when he staggered and it seemed his knees would buckle.

"It's okay, son." Harvey's voice was gentle, reassuring. "Everything's going to be all right.

I'm taking you home with me. You're going to be okay."

*　　　　*　　　　*

Eleven-year-old Billy pressed his back against the building housing Tony's Tattoo Parlor, scarcely aware of the rough brick biting through the fabric of his jacket. He was aware only of the burning in his throat as he struggled to catch his breath, the throb of his pounding heart filling his ears. Across the street, his friend Jerry and two other teenagers, sprawled, spread-eagled, across the hood of a police car. Billy's trembling knees threatened to give way. *Why were they in trouble with the police? What had they done?*

Billy was supposed to meet Jerry, and a couple of other guys Billy didn't know, outside the Pine Street Tavern at seven o'clock. Usually, whenever they got together, they just hung out, shared a joint, but tonight Jerry said they were planning to do something exciting. He wouldn't tell Billy what it was, only, if he wanted to be included, he should be there at seven. And Billy did want to be included; he wanted to be included in anything involving Jerry. Jerry was sixteen. He knew the streets of Seattle. He was the coolest guy Billy knew. Billy would be there at seven.

He planned to bug out the minute his mom left for her night job at the cannery. But, of all times, this had to be the night she decided to lay the same old lecture on him. *She didn't like him out on the streets while she was gone, she didn't like the guys he was running around with, she wished he would try to make things a little easier for her.* Well, Billy wished she'd just butt out of his life. He was old enough to take care of himself. Besides, it hadn't been his idea to move into the crummy housing development; nobody asked him how he felt about the family splitting up.

She ended up making him late with her stupid lecture. He had to sprint the fifteen blocks to the waterfront, hoping Jerry would wait for him. He spotted them, Jerry and his buddies, just as they were leaving the Third Avenue Arcade; was about to yell at them to "wait up" when the cop car careened around the corner.

Billy stared across the street to where a police officer was pulling a wad of bills from Jerry's pocket, then removing a watch from his friend's wrist before folding him into the back seat of the patrol car. *What could have happened?* Billy felt like he was going to throw up. One of the officers glanced across the street to where Billy stood. *What if the police saw him; recognized him as Jerry's friend? He had to get out of there, and fast.*

Pushing himself from the wall of cold brick, Billy flung himself back down Third Avenue, taking a left turn onto Pike Street. Rounding the corner at Second Avenue, he stumbled, almost ran right into a bunch of people, huddled at the curb. Billy could see they were trying to help some old drunk who'd fallen into the gutter. Glancing over his shoulder, expecting to see the police in hot pursuit, Billy squeezed into the knot of Good Samaritans. Hoping to hide himself in their numbers, he followed as they led the wino through the doors of the Second Avenue Mission. That was when he saw the old guy drop something into the charity box.

Billy gave up pawing through that box months ago. There was never anything in there but a lot of old, hand-me-down clothes nobody could use, or, like now, at Christmastime, a bunch of stuffed toys that didn't do anybody any good. But tonight, out of curiosity, he edged toward the box and peered over its side. He was expecting to find just an empty wine bottle, so at first, he didn't see it. Then, there it was, peeking from the folds of a pink taffeta skirt, the worn brown leather of a wallet. Billy's hands shook with excitement as, pretending to sift through the offerings, he furtively slipped the wallet beneath his jacket, then turned and darted back into the street.

Moving quickly down Second Avenue, Billy ducked into the dimly lit doorway of a pawnshop and, hunching his back toward the street, bent to examine his find. The old guy probably lifted it from some poor jerk on the street, Billy guessed. Still, there might be some money in it. Eagerly, he poked into the dark recesses of secret pockets. Nothing! Empty, except for a picture of some stupid girl smiling up at nobody.

Disappointed, Billy lifted the wallet to his nose and inhaled the musty fragrance of leather. *It sure smelled good.* It reminded him of . . . he felt a sudden stinging behind his eyelids as the image of his father forced itself into his memory. The earlier ache in the back of his throat rose again, only this time, it was different; he couldn't swallow past it. He stared down at the girl in the picture and wondered if maybe she was smiling up at her own father.

Billy's fingers tightened about the folded square of leather. He wished he could keep it, but knew he couldn't. Mom would think he'd stolen it and get all upset, probably even cry . . . like he heard her do sometimes at night when she thought he was sleeping. A funny, kind of emptiness stirred in Billy's stomach, sort of like when he was hungry, only he really wasn't hungry now. He wished somehow there was something he could do to make his mom smile again . . . like she used to.

Angrily, he tore his gaze from the object in his hand, wanting to escape the way it made him feel. He glared accusingly at the scrawny little Christmas tree in the pawnshop window, its meager adornment of glittering tinsel taunting him with the painful futility of the season. He blinked to clear away the moisture blurring his vision, then noticed a twinkling object, winking at him from beneath the branches of the little tree; a shiny beaded necklace of bright blue – his mom's favorite color.

Billy glanced down at the coveted wallet in his hand, raised it once more to inhale its heady musk, then he pushed open the door to the pawnshop.

*　　　*　　　*

Cold fingers clutching her coat tightly against the night's damp chill, Edith pressed her purse closely to her side as she hurried toward her First Avenue bus stop. She'd never overcome uneasiness at being alone in this part of town. But tonight, she was more concerned about her husband, Harvey. He'd called, just as she finished cleaning the last office. He knew her schedule by heart and often called from the phone in his cab to say "Hi", and to make sure she was okay. But tonight, he was calling from their Capitol Hill apartment to tell her he'd quit his run early. That wasn't like Harvey who always worked late on Christmas Eve.

A sigh escaped Edith's lips. Lord knows she'd tried her best to make the holidays easier for him; never making a fuss over Christmas; no decorations, no big dinner, no gifts. Edith paused at the corner of Second Avenue as the pedestrian light turned red. They should have gone back to North Dakota a long time ago. She'd wanted to; longed to embrace all those happy memories of Jimmy. But she couldn't ask Harvey to leave Seattle—the place where they'd bade their son goodbye as he went off to war. For Harvey, she knew leaving would be admitting Jimmy wasn't coming back.

The persistent supplication of a little brass bell at her elbow invaded Edith's troubled thoughts. A frown of annoyance knitting her forehead, she turned toward the uniformed Salvation Army volunteer, met his practiced smile of expectation. She didn't like opening her purse on these streets. Still, it was the very least way she could acknowledge the season of giving, if only for someone else. Releasing her hold upon her coat collar, Edith reached into her pocket, fingering the bus fare she'd placed there before leaving the office building. She hesitated only a moment before dropping her dollar into the little red pot swinging from its tripod.

The traffic light changed, sending Edith across the intersection. A frown still dug at her forehead, this time, one of consternation as she recalled the earlier phone conversation with Harvey. They were having company, he'd said; a young man would be spending Christmas with them. Her husband suggested she might want to pick up the makings for dinner on her way home. Uneasiness rested heavily on Edith's heart. It wasn't like Harvey to pick up strangers and yet . . . there had been that old familiar lilt in his voice, one she hadn't heard since . . ..

Mentally, she inventoried the food supplies in her cupboards . . . a can of string beans . . . there should be enough potatoes . . . she could stop at the Deli down the street from their apartment and pick up a canned ham, maybe even a box of cake mix. Where had she put that recipe for fudge? Unexplainably, she felt a stirring of excitement, a long-absent feeling of anticipation. Perhaps, after all, this might turn out to be good thing for Harvey.

Edith couldn't be sure what caused her to glance into the window of the pawnshop. Perhaps it was a movement behind the smudged pane of glass that captured her attention. The store proprietor was placing a newly acquired item beneath the branches of a pathetic little Christmas tree . . . a man's wallet, the exceptionally fine quality of its leather apparent even from this distance. An impulsive thought occurred to Edith, stopping her, mid-stride. A Christmas gift for their young guest . . . would she dare? She stepped to the window for closer examination and found herself gazing into the face of someone's little girl, smiling up from the wallet's picture compartment. With no more than a moment's hesitation, Edith pushed open the door and stepped into the pawnshop.

+     +     +

Young Horatius watched as the Salvation Army van pulled away from the curb, carrying with it the bell, tripod and red pot; his trademark for the past few weeks. The sigh of relief he allowed himself mingled with a tinge of regret. It was over for another season. He'd miss being a part of the holiday activity, even though this year's assignment had been a long, cold one—a station none of the other volunteers wanted. Skid Road was never a very lucrative location; he wondered why it was even worked. But tonight had been unusually gratifying. He smiled, remembering the twenty-dollar donation from that generous young soldier.

Horatius was tempted to accompany the van back to headquarters just to witness the look on the Super's face when contents of the little red pot were counted. But then, he realized no one would be hanging around the hall tonight, they'd all be heading home early to celebrate Christmas with their families. Horatius had no family, his parents deceased, his brothers and sisters scattered across the continent. His Christmas Eve would be spent sitting alone in his apartment, a thought he did not relish.

The young volunteer rubbed his hands together, hoping to restore circulation to his numbed fingers. A nice, hot cup of coffee would taste good, he decided. He glanced up the street toward the Second Avenue Mission. For some reason, he was suddenly weary of dealing with the poor, the needy, the homeless. Instead, he turned his gaze down Pine Street to where a green neon tree flickered above a dimly lit doorway. Surely, he thought, they must serve coffee at that little tavern.

"Here ya go, good buddy." The bartender shoved the cup of steaming coffee across the counter.

Horatius shrugged away the tiny gnat of annoyance threatening his composure. He detested such crass familiarity, but realized the futility of attempting to reprove it. Instead, he settled onto a stool at the bar, wrapping his cold hands around the ceramic container of hot liquid. Idly, he let his gaze wander about the room, resting for a moment on two men in plaid jackets, vehemently arguing the outcome of the war; moved on to the sailor and his girl, snuggling at one of the tables.

His attention wavered for a moment on the plump, middle-aged woman in the back booth, a shabby coat with its matted fur-collar draped loosely about her shoulders. Her hair frizzed by the damp night air, her mascara seeping down over her heavy makeup, she stared into the glass of beer in front of her. Horatius recognized the woman . . . he'd seen her many times during these past three weeks, plying her trade on the streets. He considered her a pathetic, pitiful creature, certainly too old for her chosen profession. About to look away, he heard a soft snuffling and realized, to his dismay, the woman was crying.

Horatius quickly averted his eyes, focusing for a moment upon the dark liquid in his cup, then heaved a tremulous sigh of defeat. She was, after all, one of God's children. Picking his cup up from the counter, he slid from the barstool and approached the booth.

"Excuse me, Ma'am," he murmured. "Would you mind if I sat with you to drink my coffee?"

The woman looked up in surprise, her eyes glistening with yet unshed tears. "Why, 'course not, Hon.." Her bright red lips automatically stretched into an attempted smile of invitation, only to be betrayed by a fresh surge of tears, spilling over a mascara dam, dragging its dark rivulets down her cheeks. "I . . .I'm sorry," she sniffled.

Horatius slid quietly into the seat opposite her, gently placing his comforting hand over hers. "There is no need to be sorry," he hastened. "I wish only to share a few moments of comradeship." The kindly smile he offered bore little resemblance to that of the impersonal Salvation Army volunteer. " I don't believe our Lord intended for any of us to sit alone on this holy eve of his Blessed Son's birth," he added softly.

The woman offered Horatius a sad, trembling smile. "I have a son, you know," she confided, her voice a quavering whisper. "'Course, I don't see him no more."

With the heel of her free hand, she swiped tears across her cheeks in dark, watery streaks, then her eyes softened. "I 'spect you and him'd be about the same age."

*          *          *

The young soldier lifted the brightly wrapped package from beside his plate, turning it slowly over and over in his hand. Then, smiling at the middle-aged couple seated across the table, he carefully removed the wrapping and raised the lid of a small box. A sudden gasp of surprise escaped his lips. Eyes brimming with tears, he unfolded the square of Moroccan leather to where, above the childish scrawl, "From Sissy, With Love," a little girl's familiar face smiled up at him.

# IT'S ABOUT TIME

Flattening her nose against the cold glass, Julie peered through the double-paned window, squinting to see beyond the distorted shadows dancing across its surface. But only darkness greeted her from within the office of Happy Jack's Motel. Turning her wrist, she searched the white face of her Timex. It was only eight o'clock, surely much too early to close a motel on a Friday night, unless, of course, all the rooms were rented. The glaring red vacancy sign, sizzling above her head, indicated otherwise. A frown furrowed its way between her brows. Where *was* the receptionist? And, where indeed, was her mother?

Julie felt the mercurial rise of her irritation, not only with her mother, but also with herself. By now, she should have developed immunity to her mother's endless "emergencies." Apparently, she hadn't. Why else would she be stranded in a strange city in the middle of the night, peering into the window of a closed motel. This day was turning into nothing less than a major disaster, beginning with the phone call that morning. Reluctantly, Julie raked through the ashes of their earlier conversation.

Already running late, about to close her apartment door behind her, Julie paused long enough to snatch up the jangling telephone. Assuming it was Edgar, calling to confirm their standing Saturday night dinner date, she'd been surprised to hear her mother's voice.

"Hi, Honey. I'm so glad I caught you."

"Mom? What is it? Is anything wrong? Where are you?" She'd understood, when her mother left for the Coast last week to visit her brother, Phil, it was supposedly for a two week stay.

"Oh, I'm still at Phil's. Nothing is wrong . . . except . . . I need to talk to you about something, Honey."

Frustration with her mother's usual poor timing sharpened Julie's response. "Mom, I'm just heading for the office. Can't this wait until tonight?"

"Oh, no, no, Honey, that's why I called before you left for work." There was a pause. "Why don't you come down to Phil's this weekend? We could talk then." The wheedling slipped into a sugary sweetness so familiar to Julie "It's really not something we can talk about over the phone, Honey."

"Mom . . . " Julie felt her resistance waver at the note of urgency she detected at the other end of the line.

"You could catch the bus after work and be here before nine o'clock."

"I just can't, Mom. I'm having dinner with Edgar tomorrow night."

"Oh, pooh, you can always have dinner with that old stick-in-the-mud. Julie, Honey, this is very important to me."

Julie glanced nervously at the clock, its doggedly advancing hands reminding her she was going to be late for work. "Okay, Mom," she sighed. "I'll see what I can do."

"Oh, you don't have to do anything, Sweetie." There was no mistaking the lighthearted lilt of conquest in her mother's voice. "I've already reserved a room for you at Happy Jack's Motel, right across from the bus depot. Oh, and I also made a reservation on the 5:30 Greyhound out of Seattle. Bye, bye now, Sweetie," she chirped. "Don't be late for work."

Since her tardy arrival was now unavoidable, Julie took time to toss a few essentials into an overnight bag before heading to the offices of Ketcham and Smith. Any fragile hope of arriving undetected shriveled when, slipping quietly through the office door, she discovered Mr. Smith hovering over her desk, impatiently tapping its surface with the sheaf of invoices in his hand.

*     *     *

During her coffee break, Julie put in a hasty call to Edgar at his accounting firm but, unfortunately, he was in a meeting, so she left a message for him to meet at her the Fourth Avenue Food Court for lunch. Knowing how annoyed he'd be with her for allowing herself to be manipulated again by her mother, she thought it best to explain, in person, why she was breaking their long-standing Saturday night date.

After forty-five minutes of nervously pacing the sidewalk in front of the food court, she began to wonder if Edgar had, in fact, even received her message. It wasn't like him to be late. Had there been a misunderstanding? Could he be waiting inside, she wondered. No, she distinctly remembered telling the receptionist *outside* the West entrance. She glanced up at the letters etched into the concrete arching above her. Had she said the "West entrance," or just "outside the entrance?" Could he possibly be waiting at the East entrance? The watch on her wrist told her it was now ten minutes to one. She dared not repeat this morning's transgression. She'd have to wait and call him when she got to the motel.

*     *     *

She'd been forced to forego lunch, there'd not been time for dinner; she'd barely made it to the depot in time to board the 5:30 bus. Now, as she stood glaring into the darkened motel office, her neglected stomach rumbled its disfavor. She glanced toward the friendly lights beckoning from the village. Maybe she could find a restaurant, or at least a phone, where she could call Uncle Phil. Grasping the motel doorknob to give it one more hopeful jiggle, she noticed a little white slip of paper taped high up on the door panel; her name, "Julie Johnston," scrawled across it. She peeled the tiny missive from its makeshift bulletin board and carefully unfolded it.

"You are booked in room 6A," the large loopy letters informed her. "The key is under the mat. Room rate is $8.00 per night, minimum two nights. If no one is in the office when you check out, put the key under the mat and leave the money in the Bible." It was merely signed, "The Management."

Well, certainly not what you'd expect from a four star property, Julie thought. But it was convenient to the bus depot. Making her way along the row of doors until she came to room 6A, Julie stooped and lifted the scruffy straw doormat. Sure enough, there was the key, just as promised. Turning it in the lock, she entered the dim room and, groping along the wall, flipped on the light switch. No, she decided, certainly not a "four star," but at least it was clean.

She'd dropped her bag onto the bed before she spied the envelope lying at her feet, apparently slipped beneath the door sometime earlier. She recognized her mother's hand in the neatly printed letters. "Julie, come to the China Seas Restaurant when you get in. Two blocks north of the motel. Turn left on Alder. Next door to Phil's book store. We'll meet you there about 8:30." At this moment, any restaurant was an ideal place to meet, thought Julie. Pulling a sweater from her overnight case, she turned toward the door, then hesitating, glanced at her mother's note. "*We'll* meet you there?" Uncle Phil . . .of course, who else? Still, an unexplainable uneasiness fluttered in her stomach. Just hunger, she decided, pulling the door shut behind her.

Julie made short work of her cup of egg flower soup and was eagerly attacking the savory offerings of a Number Three Dinner for One, when the unmistakable, giddy trill of her mother's voice blatantly invaded the room. Looking up, Julie felt her throat tighten, refusing passage to the forkful of Mu Gu Gai Pan she had just slipped into her mouth.

Chiffon scarf floating behind her, stiletto heels clicking upon the tile floor, the familiar petite figure of her mother swooped across the room.

But it was not the sight of her mother's flamboyant appearance creating Julie's breathing problem. More so, it was the "we", or rather the "he", following in her wake. Behind her, crisp, dark hair falling carelessly over his forehead, broad muscular shoulders straining against the tight-fitting T shirt tucked into slim-waisted, faded jeans, was a man half her mother's age. Tanned skin that literally glistened, eyes permanently crinkled at the corners, suggested hours of exposure to the summer sun. Julie cringed inwardly. So, this was the subject too important to discuss over the phone.

Gulping a mouthful of hot green tea to clear her throat, Julie rose to accept her mother's exuberant hug while casting a scowl toward the gigalo who would seduce her mother, if he hadn't already done so. A pair of twinkling, sea-green eyes unflinchingly met her accusing glare—one dark eyebrow lifted quizzically.

Planting a faux kiss on Julie's cheek, the older woman turned toward her young man, pulling him closer to her side. "Antonio, this is my beautiful daughter I've been telling you about. And Julie, this is Antonio, Antonio Babucino."

Her mother's companion flashed a most disarming smile, his even white teeth startling in their contrast to his bronzed skin. "Tony," he corrected, "Just Tony."

Julie's breath caught in her throat as the soft baritone voice crowded past her anger, sending an unexpected tremor shuddering down the nape of her neck. Quickly lowering her eyes, she glowered at the cooling rice congealing upon her plate. *Charleton! He needn't waste his charms on her!*

Although he remained standing, Tony pulled out a chair for Julie's mother, whose unceasing chatter continued to swirl about them.

"It was so lucky I was in the bookstore last Tuesday when Antonio came in. Of all things, he was looking for something to read while his boat was being repaired," she babbled. "With Phil working every day, I'd have been utterly bored to tears if it weren't for Antonio. He's been such a dear."

*I'll just be he has,* Julie wanted to retort. Instead, she forced a tight smile to her lips. "How nice," she replied stiffly, while her mind floundered for some way to overthrow this brazen Lothario.

"My boat'll be out of the hospital tomorrow." That smile again. "I promised Vera . . . your mother . . . I'd take the two of you for a spin around the bay, that is, if it's agreeable with you."

Julie's curt refusal was cut short by a cry of despair from her mother. "Oh, Antonio," Vera wailed in her sweetest little girl voice. "I'm so sorry. I meant to tell you. Phil offered to take tomorrow off and drive me over to see my friend, Martha." Then her pout disappeared and her face brightened as if an idea suddenly occurred to her. "But there's no reason the two of you can't go. I'm sure Antonio won't mind," she purred. "Would you, Antonio?"

"My pleasure." The words rumbled from deep within the young man's throat. "Now, if you ladies will excuse me, I've some cleaning up to do on the boat." He turned to Julie. "I'll pick you up in the morning, then, at your motel . . . the Happy Jack is it, say, about ten?"

In stunned silence, Julie stared after him as Tony, not waiting for her response, turned on his heel and strode from the room. She scarcely heard her mother bubbling on about "that nice young man." For the second time, the Mu Gu Gai Pan rose threateningly to the back of Julie's throat as a hot wave of humiliating realization washed over her. Tony was not her mother's new boyfriend, but just another hapless victim in Vera's never-ending match making efforts. She steadfastly refused to accept the existence of Edgar, who she considered to be an unsuitable consort for her only daughter.

Julie felt her fury building inside her. Mildly innocuous until now, this time her mother's meddling had gone too far. Struggling to control her anger, she turned to the woman beside her. "Mother, we need to talk."

"Oh, dear, look at the time. It's almost nine o'clock," gasped the would-be matchmaker, glancing at the diamond-encrusted timepiece on her slender wrist. "Phil will be closing the book store and wanting to start home. I mustn't keep him waiting." She rose quickly to her feet. "We'll talk later, Sweetie. I promise." Fluttering her hand in an airy wave of dismissal, Vera scurried from the restaurant, leaving Julie with only the remains of her Number Three Dinner to glower at, the Mu Gu Gai Pan now an unappealing blob upon her plate, the pot of green tea, grown tepid.

*How could she?* Julie fumed inwardly. *How dared she?* Admittedly, her relationship with Edgar was not an especially exciting one, but it was . . . well . . . predictable. Dinner out every Saturday night, Monday night sports on the TV, a quiet game of scrabble every Wednesday—dull, perhaps by her mother's standards, but the choice was not her mother's. Tonight's fiasco was the final straw. If she let her mother get away with this latest, most audacious, intrusion into her life, Julie knew she would never have peace again.

*       *       *

It was 9:30 the following morning when Julie tucked a twenty-dollar bill into the Gideon Bible, slid the square door key beneath the mat and slipped out of room 6A of Happy Jack's Motel. The off ice was dark and empty when she crossed the street to the bus depot and climbed aboard the 9:45 bus headed for Seattle.

Stuffing her bag onto the overhead rack, Julie settled herself into a third row window seat when she caught sight of the dark-haired, jean-clad figure striding up the sidewalk, his easy, rolling gait that of a man accustomed to navigating the unsteady decks of a boat. Recognition brought with it, a sudden twinge of guilt. Tony! She'd forgotten to leave him a note. She half rose then sank back into her seat. *No, this was Mother's doing. Let her take the consequences.*

Julie quickly averted her eyes to where, on the opposite side of the street, boats inside the marina bobbed impatiently in their slips as if eager, on such a beautiful day, to be out skimming across the waters of the bay where sea green waters twinkled in the sun like . . .. For some reason, recollection of a pair of twinkling, sea green eyes flashed before Julie. She quickly lifted her attention skyward, away from the tantalizing memory. Screeching seagulls swooped above the wharf, intimidating their peers for possession of a coveted scrap of garbage. Pungent saltwater odors of kelp and fish, hovering above the waterfront, crept into the interior of the departing bus, bound for Seattle. A wistful sigh escaped Julie's lips.

Resolutely, she turned her attention toward the road ahead where green and white signs announced their approach to the freeway onramp. She studied the white face of her Timex. She should arrive at her Seattle destination in plenty of time for her Saturday night dinner date with Edgar. This was the third Saturday of the month; which would mean, of course, they'd be dining Mexican. As usual, he'd probably already chosen the restaurant and made reservations without consulting her. It was a good thing she put off calling him from the motel last night. It might be a good idea to call him now, just to confirm the time. He had such a fetish about promptness. Besides, he was already going to be upset when he learned about her latest surrender to her mother's manipulation.

Another, heavier sigh, slipped past Julie's lips. This most recent escapade was certain to dominate the conversation, albeit a one sided one, during the coming Monday night football, Tuesday night scrabble and possibly even into next week's dinner date when, being the fourth Saturday, they'd, of course, be dining Chinese.

As she pulled the cell phone from her purse, a white slip of paper fluttered to the seat beside her. She was about to stuff it back into her handbag when her eyes fell upon its message, slid across the carelessly scribbled words: "The key is under the mat . . . Minimum two nights . . . Leave the money in the Bible."

*The key is under the mat.*

Julie glanced back over her shoulder to where tall masts of sailboats bobbled restlessly above the awakening marina.

There was perhaps the tiniest fraction of a moment's hesitation before Julie's hand shot upward, reaching for the overhead emergency cord that would stop the 9:45 a.m. bus headed for Seattle.

# ONE SMALL CANDLE

Vladimir glanced at his wrist where normally his father's handsome gold timepiece would have revealed the hour of the day. But, of course, the watch was gone now, as was his suitcase and the fifty dollars pinned inside his jacket. Vladimir directed his gaze to where the sun drifted midway between its zenith and the western horizon. It was perhaps three, or three thirty, he guessed. It must have been close to noon, then, when he fell off the produce truck, although, thinking back, he wondered if maybe he hadn't been pushed.

\*　　　\*　　　\*

The thought of his Poppa and Mamma; the wife and two little children, depending upon him to rescue them from the struggle to survive in a country strife with economic upheaval, was what kept him from turning back those first few days. All too fresh in his mind were the months of hardship they endured, selling precious produce and worthless souvenirs from the roadside in order to buy his passage to America. Still vivid in his memory was the day he said goodbye to his little family. His father, although still hopeful for the return of the old, less stressful regime, gave Vladimir his blessing, then strapped his treasured watch onto his son's wrist with the admonition "In your new job you must have a good watch. You will need always to be on time."

At that moment, Vladimir vowed he'd not fail his family and their faith in him.

He'd chosen to board a cargo ship headed for Canada where entry permits were easier to obtain. From there, he planned to cross into America on foot. The first part of his journey went smoothly; he was able to go ashore at the Canadian seaport without incident. However, the road to the border proved to be a long and dusty one; his battered suitcase, though lightly packed, grew heavy—the split plastic of its handle gouging blisters in his palms. As his destination grew nearer, he began to have concerns over the fallibility of his plan. Could he successfully slip across the border, undetected? And if not, just how strict were they? So immersed in his dilemma, he was scarcely aware of the produce truck until it pulled alongside him.

The unshaven passenger, seated next to the equally unkempt driver of the truck, leaned out the open window. "Need a ride, Rube?" He offered Vladimir a tobacco stained grin.

The sudden surge of relief Vladimir felt was indescribable. "Oh, yes," he responded eagerly. "That would be most welcomed." He lost no time in accepting the invitation as the driver waved him onto the back of the truck. Tossing his suitcase before him, he swung onto the flatbed where two young men were already perched atop crates filled with turnips, beets and rutabagas.

Vladimir smiled in greeting. The younger man raked Vladimir with his disdainful gaze, then elbowing the man beside him, muttered a few words under his breath. The laughter that followed was loud and abrasive. It was obvious to Vladimir they were laughing at him. Perhaps it was his ill-fitting, hand-me-down suit, too small for his large-boned frame, or the unkempt coarseness of his dark hair, grown long and shaggy from the past few weeks of neglect. Having little understanding of the language, he could not know. Turning his back to them, he reached for the suitcase lying at his feet. As he tucked it between the crates of turnips, the too-short sleeve of his jacket crawled up his arm, exposing the watch strapped to his wrist. The young man whispered into the ear of his companion, but there was no laughter this time.

They traveled several miles in silence with only occasional whispers shared between the two men. Vladimir made no attempt to communicate with his fellow travelers. He would have liked to question them regarding their destination, perhaps learn more of the procedure in crossing the border, but concentrated, instead, upon the countryside flashing past them. He was, perhaps, the first to notice their approach to the cluster of buildings straddling the highway and, once again, the knot of nervousness tightened within his chest. It could only be the border station.

This was not as he planned—it was his intent to slip into America on foot, unnoticed, not on a produce truck where, undoubtedly, he would be questioned for his entry papers. Perhaps he should seek the attention of the driver, ask to be let off the truck before it reached the border.

"Hey, Rube." The young man's harsh voice commanded Vladimir's attention. "You got a green card?"

Sensing Vladimir's confusion, his harasser continued. "You could be in a lot of trouble with the authorities up ahead, crossing the border without a green card." A lascivious sneer curved his lips. "Tell you what, we'll keep quiet if you make it worth our while."

They were nearing the border station. Vladimir could taste the bile of fear rising in the back of his throat. "But, I have no money."

"That watch of yours will do. Give us the watch and we'll keep our mouths shut."

*No! Not his father's watch!* Vladimir saw again the pride in his father's face as he presented his son with the precious timepiece. He saw, too, the hope and loving trust softening the face of his wife. He closed his eyes, visualizing his two small children, Natasha and Valery, knew the warmth he always felt at their presence, the sadness always filling him at the absence of little Ana, lost to them when there was no money to fight the winter sickness. Reluctantly, he unfastened the watch and handed it to his tormentor, watched in painful silence as the man strapped it onto his own wrist.

There was no incident at the border station. Scarcely daring to breathe, Vladimir hunched down among the boxes of produce. But the officers made no attempt to stop the truck, shouting greetings to the driver as they waved him through the gate. Only then did Vladimir realize this was no doubt a regular run for these farmers on their way to market, there was no need to repeatedly examine their papers. He'd been duped, relinquished his father's treasured timepiece for no reason. Chagrined, but seeing no possible recourse for the turn of events, he silently exchanged his place of hiding for a position atop a crate of lettuce. From there, he would have a view of the roadway ahead and could watch for a suitable place to disembark.

It was from this sentinel position, he was rewarded with his first glimpse of an American city. The sight of tall stately buildings, reaching into the heavens, their expansive windows flashing its bright reflection back to the sun, brought Vladimir to his feet. His face flushed with the excitement surging through him, all his misgivings melted as this awesome mecca of opportunity seemed to open its arms in welcome. It was at that very moment the truck suddenly lurched and, thrown off balance, Vladimir tumbled from the truck bed, landing on his shoulder on the pavement below. Scrambling to his feet, he shouted after the retreating vehicle, then watched helplessly as it disappeared down the street, his battered suitcase still tucked among the crates of produce. With heavy heart, Vladimir realized he had little choice but to walk the remaining distance into the city.

*         *         *

Although he had not yet reached the center of the metropolis, Vladimir was amazed at the number of people passing him along the sidewalk. Uncertainty halted his footsteps. Where was he to go now, what was he to do next? Across the street, he noticed a small, grass-covered park, its green leafy trees shading an occasional small bench. Perhaps he could rest there a moment, he thought, at least until he could decide what he must do.

Wearily, he lowered himself onto the wooden slats of his chosen bench. The first problem he faced was to find a place to stay for the night. Reaching inside his jacket, he released the crinkled paper notes pinned there. Carefully, he fingered the green bills, while his mind sought to re-calculate the value of the unfamiliar currency.

Captive of his concentration, it was a moment before he became aware of someone standing in front of him. Raising his eyes, he discovered a thin young woman, dressed in faded blue jeans and a shapeless brown jacket, staring down at him. The chalk-whiteness of her face, framed by a mat of limp, unkempt hair, accentuated her expressionless eyes, the deep, dark circles underling them. Beside her, clutching the hem of the woman's soiled brown jacket, was a small child Vladimir guessed to be about three years old.

"Oh, please, can you spare a few dollars? My children are hungry and I have no job," the woman pleaded, her words tumbling over one another in their haste to be heard. "If you could spare me just a few dollars. It's for my children."

Vladimir looked at the child staring up at him from large, liquid brown eyes, and a painful lump filled his throat. He knew what it was like to watch your children go hungry, to helplessly stand by as your small daughter succumbed to the winter sickness because there was no money for medicine. Vladimir extended his hand holding the folded green bills.

"How much will you need?" he asked softly. Then, as the woman's trembling fingers snatched the bills from his hand, "No, no, please not all. It is all I have."

"I will not spend it all." The woman's voice grew sharp. "I'll bring you back the change. I promise. Here," she pushed the child forward. "She will stay with you until I come back. I will come back. I promise." And then, she was gone, scurrying across the green grass and down the sidewalk.

It was now nearly six o'clock. The woman had not returned. Vladimir glanced toward the child, seated quietly beside him. She had not stirred or spoken since the woman left, only casting an occasional glance toward Vladimir, her wide brown eyes clouded with apprehension.

Surely, a mother would not abandon such a little one, thought Vladimir. Despair stung the backs of his eyelids. What was he to do? What of his poor family back in Russia? Had he failed them this day with his stupidity? And this child, he agonized, what of her? He could perhaps survive by himself, but he could not leave this child. Where were they to sleep? How were they to eat on what few coins remained in his pocket?

He remembered, then, the orange he was saving for his evening meal. Pulling it from his pocket, he painstakingly removed the thick, orange skin. Carefully dividing the segments into two equal parts, he extended one portion toward the child. Her small hand darted out, quickly claiming ownership of the fruit that disappeared almost immediately, leaving no trace but a small rivulet of juice, dribbling from the corner of her mouth. With a sigh of resignation, Vladimir extended his own half of the orange. The brown eyes softened and a ghost of a smile flitted across the pale little lips as his small companion slowly reached out to accept Vladimir's offering.

The sun was dipping behind the trees, releasing an impatient evening chill from the damp earth. Shrugging out of his jacket, Vladimir draped it about the child's thin shoulders. "First, little one, we must find us a place to sleep this night." Vladimir's voice was gentle. "And then tomorrow . . .." He shrugged. "Well, tomorrow is tomorrow."

He felt its soft warmth as the little girl's small hand slipped timidly into his and, suddenly, the image of another little girl flashed across his mind. He was seeing, again, the inscription he'd laboriously carved into Ana's tiny gravestone: *"There is not enough darkness in all the world to put out the light of one small candle."* Vladimir looked down into the trusting brown eyes gazing up at him and a gentle smile lifted the corners of his mouth.

"Do not be afraid, little one." His fingers tightened about the tiny hand he held in his own. "Together, you and I, we will find our way."

*          *          *

The threatening darkness of approaching night turned a defensive city into a blazing fortress of white lights. Vladimir now carried the tired little girl in the crook of his arm, her head resting on his shoulder, the warmth of her gentle breathing caressing his neck. Like a hungry mongrel, despair nipped at his heels as he trudged the unfriendly streets. He turned his thoughts from the ache of hunger twisting in his belly, knowing her own hunger would soon awaken the child. But, that problem would have to belong to tomorrow. Tonight, he must find them refuge. He thought of the few coins nested in his pocket, scarcely enough for either food or lodging. While he stubbornly rejected the bleak alternative of a sheltered doorway as their night's haven, it began to appear the choice would not be his.

Immersed in the painful reality of his dilemma, his attention focused hopefully upon the kaleidoscope of glittering marquees ahead, Vladimir was startled as an apparently inebriated man, almost colliding with him, stumbled past them. Quickly stepping into the comparative safety of a doorway, Vladimir glanced at the sign overhead, illuminated by one single light bulb…Second Avenue Mission. A tiny moth of hope fluttered in his chest. *Was not a mission a place of refuge for the needy?*

While the building was not the most appealing edifice lining the sidewalk—its double wooden doors scarred from age, graffiti marring its faded brick front—the light shining through the smudged glass of a small window was a like beautiful beacon of salvation for Vladimir. Hesitating no more than an instant, he stepped through the double doors. He found himself facing a room, though not overly large, obviously being utilized as an eating area, its limited space filled with long rows of narrow dining tables.

"Welcome to our mission." Vladimir turned toward the soft voice. "How can we be of help to you?" An older woman, of perhaps sixty or sixty-five years of age, stood at his elbow. The warmth in her bright blue eyes mirrored the friendliness of her greeting.

"We need shelter for tonight," Vladimir began, then paused. "But, I have no money."

"That is not a problem. All are welcome here." Her smile was gentle. "I believe we have the perfect spot for you, two beds down at the end of the sleeping hall." She indicated a door at the far end of the room. "A quiet corner for you and the child."

The little girl stirred on Vladimir's arm, a small whimper escaping her lips. The frown scurrying across the woman's face was replaced by the return of her gentle smile. "Perhaps, before I take you to your beds, you would like come into the kitchen with me. The dinner hour is over but I'm sure we can bend the rules a little."

Tears stung the back of his eyelids. "You are most kind," Vladimir murmured. "I do not have a job yet, but when I find one, I will most surely repay you for your kindness."

"You must not concern yourself with such things tonight," the woman insisted. "Tomorrow, when you have rested, we will see, then, what perhaps we can to do to help you find that job," she raised her eyebrows, " Mr. . . . Mr. . . .?"

"Vladimir . . . I am called Vladimir."

"And your daughter?"

Vladimir stared blankly at the woman.

"Your little girl, what is her name?"

Vladimir glanced down at the sleeping child snuggled in his arms. He hesitated a moment. "Ana," he whispered softly. "Her name is Ana."

# IF THERE WERE NO BIRTHDAYS

Giving one last futile tug at the once loose-fitting over-blouse now clinging snuggly to the plumpness of her hips, Sarah consulted the Timex strapped to her wrist. Twelve forty-five—still plenty of time before the one-thirty meeting of the Friday afternoon bridge club. She smoothed her hands over the lately-too-tight skirt stretching across her abdomen. Maybe she should change into her seersucker with the boxy jacket. "Oh, what the heck," she dismissed the idea with a careless shrug. She was as ready as she was going to get. In fact, she decided she might just as well leave now—shock Alice by being early; Alice with her irritating fetish for time schedules. Annoyance stretched Sarah's lips into a thin, petulant line. In her opinion, it had been a huge mistake appointing over-bearing Alice Worton as their new committee chairman—she had been against it from the beginning.

Digging the car keys from its innards, Sarah tucked her purse beneath her arm, glancing automatically into the hall mirror as she passed through the entryway. In deference to habit, she paused, dutifully fluffing the graying wisps of hair lying limply against her forehead; fastidiously flicking away the speck of eye makeup smudging her cheek. She reached for the doorknob, then, hesitating, turned back toward the tired reflection staring at her from the shiny, smooth glass. She frowned, peering into those weary features scowling back at her, as if seeing them for the first time.

Dark circles underlined hooded eyes; once sparkling with an enthusiasm for life, now gazing at her from behind the dull veil of listlessness. A web of tiny lines, splaying outward from the corners of those eyes, etched their way down once-firm cheeks now lying in lazy pouches along her jaw line. Sarah raised her fingers to her face, slowly traced the creases parenthesizing her mouth. When had she grown so old? A sigh of resignation slipped past Sarah's lips. "Time, such a thief you are," she whispered.

A rebellious frown dug into her forehead. When had she succumbed to this misnomer of the "golden years", accepted the boring choreographed existence of retirement—each day a carbon copy of the last? A tiny moth of discontent fluttered in her chest. Is this what she wanted, she asked herself, to slip from life on the greased runway of mediocrity; a few apathetic years before sinking listlessly into the quagmire of old age? What was it the speaker at last week's luncheon had asked—"If there were no birthdays to give number to the years, how old would you be?"

A spark of defiance tightened Sarah's jaw, deepening the scowl across her face. "Just as old as I want to be," she enlightened her lethargic reflection. "After all, I'm only sixty-eight years old, still have my health." But where to begin, the frowning image challenged? A frantic search into her storeroom of faded memories resurrected dusty recollections of earlier days when the excitement of travel had been the pearl in her oyster. *Well, it could be again!*

Casting one last glare toward the old woman in the mirror, Sarah turned on her heel and stomped into the living room, Alice's rigid time schedule no longer a concern. Slamming her purse onto the coffee table, Sarah snatched up the recently discarded copy of the daily news and turned to the Travel section.

+          +          +

Hovering uneasily inside the doorway of the airline terminal, Sarah nervously eyed the long queue of travelers inching their way to the ticket counter through a maze of roped off channels crisscrossing the terminal floor. For one moment of uncertainty, she contemplated dashing back into the street, reclaiming the taxi she'd just left, and returning to the safe haven of her small apartment. She was appalled at the overwhelming number of travelers since she'd last set foot in an airport. Air travel seemed so much less intimidating then . . . when was it, certainly not that long ago, when she'd taken the trip to Phoenix to visit her high school friend? How could things have changed so much? She tried to recall the phone conversation of a week ago when she'd made the reservations. She was simply told to pick up her boarding pass at the airport, but could remember nothing—nothing at all, being offered to prepare her for this unexpected anthill of activity.

"Oh, for Pete's sake, Sarah," she hissed. "Get a grip."

She could either enter this long line twisting its arduous way to the ticket counter where her boarding pass awaited, or stand here like a bump on a log and miss her flight. Dragging a desperate breath of courage into her lungs, Sarah tightened her fingers on the handle of her suitcase and stepped forward.

Joining what she couldn't resist comparing to a restless herd of cattle being funneled down the confines of a chute, Sarah shuffled her way along with the milling, impatient throng of hopefuls. Scooting her suitcase ahead of her with the toe of her shoe; at the same time restraining the narrow strap of her handbag, insistent upon slipping from her left shoulder, she struggled to ease the pressure of her suddenly too-heavy carry-on, its strap now digging painfully into her right shoulder. Finally, just when the pain in her arm subsided into wooden-like numbness, it was her turn at the counter. Gratefully, she allowed the carry-on to slip from her shoulder. Managing a pleasant, if insincere, smile, she groped awkwardly in her handbag until the fingers of her desensitized right hand located the scrap of paper bearing the confirmation notes she'd scribbled during last week's phoned-in booking.

A stone-faced agent glanced at the reservation data, then, with a careless wave of her hand, wordlessly directed Sarah's attention to a small electronic device attached to the counter at the right of the ticket window.

The weak smile slid from Sarah's lips as she suspiciously eyed the unfamiliar contraption in front of her. Turning back to the agent, she could only shrug her shoulders, shaking her head in bewilderment. "I'm sorry, I don't . . . .."

"Just punch in your flight information." A tinge of impatience shadowed the terse response.

Sarah refocused upon her mechanical nemesis, staring blankly at the rows of mystically labeled buttons confronting her. She hadn't the vaguest clue as to what was expected of her. Fortunately, at that moment, a kindhearted young person at an identical station beside her, apparently sensing Sarah's confusion, reached across the device and pointed at one button.

"Punch that and follow the directions," the teenager smiled. "It'll tell you what to do."

*Name, Destination, Airline, Flight number, Number of passengers, Any weapons in your possession?*

Sarah fumbled through the dispassionate inquisition, hesitantly pressing indicated buttons until, at last, surprised at the surge of pride she experienced, held her own self-produced boarding pass in hand. The glow of achievement was quickly dissipated, however.

"Check in at Gate D," was the brusquely delivered command urging her on to the security station, its series of stern-faced officials and what proved to be her first step into an even more hectic haze of chaos.

*May I see your boarding pass? Your ID, please. Any firearms, sharp weapons, drugs, bottles containing liquid? Move along. Move along. Place all metal objects and jewelry in this basket, please. Take off your coat, please. You are required to remove your shoes. May I see your boarding pass? Please, place your purse on the conveyor belt. Please, step through the security screen. Move along, please.* Hurry, hurry— shuffle, shuffle. *Isn't this your coat? Don't forget your purse.* "Excuse me, that's my carry-on." *Please, move along. You can put your shoes on, over there, in that chair.* Oh, guess not, *someone else has taken it. Move along. Please, go directly to your gate. Do not leave your baggage unattended.*

Feet jammed into unlaced shoes, wadded coat stuffed beneath the strap of her carry-on, Sarah floundered along the concourse, scrutinizing the rows of illuminated boxes overhead. There it was, Gate 17, designated departure gate for flight 423, the flight number printed on her hard-won boarding pass. With a sigh, she sank into one of the less-than-comfortable metal chairs facing the plate glass windows, grateful to be out of the madhouse she'd just been through—for the chance get reorganized. The edges of the carefully pre-woven tapestry of her day, once viewed with anticipation, were quickly fraying, along with her endurance. Thankfully, she sighed, nothing to do now but wait, wait until her flight was announced. Wait. And wait. What wouldn't she give for a cup of coffee? Best not to leave, though, she decided nervously, with the flight scheduled to take off any minute.

The address system crackled overhead, shrill instructions swarming into the room.

*Flight 423 has been delayed. Passengers will please check the monitor for rescheduled flight time. Do not leave your bags unattended*

Sarah stared helplessly at the disarray of personal possessions gathered at her feet.

*The departure gate for Flight 423 has been changed. Flight 423 will now be departing from Gate 12. Please, check the monitor for departure time. Do not leave your bags unattended.*

Once again the strap of the carry-on was cutting into her shoulder, her suitcase nipping at her heels, her dangling purse swatting the back of her knees, as Sarah staggered to Gate 12—took her place in the line of agitated humanity.

*Flight 423 is now loading.* Once again the dispassionate voice shrilled its commands. *First class passengers only may now board. All rows are now boarding. Please, have your boarding pass ready. Please, keep moving.*

Struggling down the narrow aisle, Sarah fervently wished, for the hundredth time, she'd chosen to pay the extra fee for checking her bag rather than opting to drag it with her. At this moment, it had become such an albatross she would have gleefully welcomed its banishment to the lost luggage department if given the slightest opportunity.

*All bags must be stored in overhead compartments or beneath the seat in front of you. Please, keep moving.*

Sarah peered at her now crumpled boarding pass, finally able to confirm her assigned seat number with its matching component displayed above the row beside her. Fortunately, her carry-on would fit nicely beneath the seat, she decided, but hefting the large, bulky suitcase would require agility long since stealthily siphoned from her by the passing years. Dropping her carry-on onto the seat, she strained against the resisting bit of luggage at her feet.

*All bags must be stored in an overhead compartment. Please, do not block the aisle.*

Sarah felt her stomach knot with frustration, her fingers cramp, as she awkwardly forced one knee beneath the cumbersome bit of baggage.

"May I put that in the overhead for you?" The deep male-voiced inquiry coming from over her shoulder couldn't have been more welcomed were it the voice of St Peter, offering unconditional absolution of all her sins. Turning toward the speaker, Sarah found herself looking up into the pleasant face of a gentleman she would have guessed to be—should she be pressed to put a number to his years—in his early seventies. His friendly smile slashed its way between the soft canopy of a gray mustache on his upper lip and the neatly trimmed goatee covering his chin. Her shoulders sagging in defeat, a tiny whimper of relief escaped Sarah's lips.

One shaggy gray, male eyebrow arched quizzically above twinkling blue eyes. "Can I take that for a 'yes'?"

"Oh, yes," Sarah gasped weakly, relinquishing her hold upon the handle of the unwieldy bit of baggage. "Yes, please."

*Please, keep moving. Please, do not block the aisle.*

With ease belying his obvious years, her elderly benefactor hefted her luggage into the overhead rack while Sarah, obeying the persistent voice of the loud speaker, quickly squeezed out of the aisle and into the narrow compartment. Dropping her carry-on onto the floor, she kicked it beneath the seat in front of her, then slipped into the confining seventeen inches of seating being allotted her. Fastening the seat belt snuggly across her lap, she glanced up to where her elderly Samaritan still lingered, now intent upon comparing the numbers on his own boarding pass with those posted above the seats.

Then, to her surprise, he lowered himself into the cushioned chair beside her. "Well, now, isn't this a pleasant stroke of luck?" he announced with a smile. "It looks like you and I are going to be traveling companions."

Her momentary euphoria of deliverance evaporated. *Oh, good grief,* Sarah agonized inwardly. *Am I ready for this?* Grudgingly aware of the verbal participation expected from her during the next few hours, she managed a polite facsimile of anticipated pleasure in response. "Yes, it does, doesn't it?" she murmured.

A tiny gremlin of uneasiness nudged aside her annoyance as she quickly assessed the gentleman seated next to her. For some reason, she found his debonair, almost cavalier demeanor, somehow disturbing. What was it about him that bothered her?

Well, no mind, the trip would eventually be over. It was a relief just to finally be aboard the plane . . . to finally be on her way. Her searching fingers found and depressed the button on the arm of her chair, releasing the seat into a reclining position. With a sigh, she leaned into the questionable comfort of the hard-backed cushion, closed her eyes and surrendered herself to exhaustion. From the brink of somnolence, she heard the bang, bang, snap as overhead compartments were secured. The next moment, a commanding voice startled her back to reality.

"All seats are to be in an upright position for take-off, Ma'am," scolded the uniformed young woman hovering above Sarah, an admonishing frown suggesting no tolerance for anything less than immediate compliance.

"Yes, yes, of course." Sarah's groping fingers, fumbling across the smooth surface of the arm of her chair in a hasty search for the release button, encountered another, quicker, set of fingers. The back of her seat, unexpectedly freed from restraint, jolted forward, hurtling her into a sudden upright position.

"Thank you, Sir." The attendant smiled sweetly at the accommodating gray-haired passenger seated next to Sarah, who then turned toward her, no doubt anticipating her approval as well.

Lips pressed tightly together, Sarah forced what she hoped would pass for a smile of gratitude and not the grimace reflecting her annoyance. Apparently her hypocritical efforts were successful for the gentleman responded with a magnanimous smile of his own.

"No problem, little lady," he reassured her. "Glad to be of service."

Maintenance of a gracious smile became more difficult as Sarah's jaws clenched together tightly, imprisoning the insolent retort clawing at the back of her throat. *Little lady, indeed! And who asked for his but-insky service, anyway? She was absolutely capable of taking care of herself.* Fortunately, Sarah's irritation was diverted as the flight attendant commandeered her attention toward the front of the plane, saving her from perhaps launching an ill-advised counter attack upon her self-appointed guardian.

"In case of an emergency, an oxygen mask will drop down." The face covering was held up for their inspection. "You will immediately secure it over your nose and mouth." The young woman then deftly demonstrated the proper procedure for donning the life-saving device. The following, impassive recitation of the numerous, carefully contrived features installed to insure the safety of their flight, reminded Sarah that some things about air travel hadn't changed.

The dutifully rendered dissertation complete, the stewardess returned to her seat and a few moments later, the engines screamed their commitment; the plane shuddered, like a restless Pegasas pawing the earth, impatient to take flight. From her window, Sarah watched the buildings drift away, the runway move swiftly beneath as they picked up speed and then, that familiar moment of fear, the tightening in the pit of her stomach, as the ground suddenly dropped from her vision and they were airborne. She hadn't realized how tightly she'd been gripping the arms of her seat until she felt the warmth of another's hand over her white-knuckled one. Startled, she glanced from the tanned fingers covering hers into the concerned countenance of her improbable traveling companion.

"You okay, little lady?" A smile of reassurance contradicted the troubled concern clouding his blue eyes.

Sarah snatched her hand from the intimidating enclosure, felt her palms dampen with the uneasy discomfiture at this unwelcome solicitous advance. "Yes, yes, of course. I'm fine," she stammered. "Really, I'm okay."

The lump of constriction in Sarah's stomach, usually dissipating moments after take-off, now took on greater proportions, creating a Gregorian knot of nervous apprehension which threatened to disgorge the healthy breakfast she'd forced upon herself that morning.

*What was with this guy, anyway? Was he trying to hit on her?*

*Oh, for crying out loud, Sarah*, she chided herself. *You're behaving like a paranoid teenager. Face it, you're a slightly plump, over-the-hill, sixty-eight year old matron; surely not someone apt to inspire romantic overtures, even from an aging Lothario.* Although, casting a furtive glance in the direction of her traveling companion, Sarah did have to admit he was rather handsome for a man of his years. Self-consciously, she smoothed her hands over her hair, hoping to restore her dislodged coiffure; her fingertips automatically fussing at the limp strands of gray hair clinging to her forehead.

Sarah glanced at her watch, suddenly anxious for this flight to be over. One thirty—Alice would be orchestrating the bridge club program about now. A twinge of regret pricked at her conscience along with a sudden longing for the security of routine, the comfort of the predictable.

Hoping to discourage any further attempt at interaction from her companion, Sarah once again depressed the armchair button, releasing her seat into a reclining position. Lying back, she closed her eyes, surrendering to their soothing monotony as the steady hum of the plane's engines lulled her into a welcomed state of drowsiness.

*          *          *

Her euphoria, however, was destined to be short-lived. Sarah wasn't sure how long she'd slept when a sudden jolt jarred her into wakefulness. Her startled gaze witnessed, first, the frenzied blinking of the overhead lights, then the row of flickering tiny white lights racing excitedly down either side of the aisle. Her sleep befuddled brain groped frantically for an elusive bit of recent input, which suddenly seemed extremely important to recall. The stewardess—what did she say about the row of lights along the aisle? They would light up during an emergency . . . an emergency? Another sharp jolt, accompanied by a searing flash of light, sent Sarah's heart ricocheting into her throat. Outbursts of surprise and panic erupted among the passengers before an intercom crackled overhead, interrupting their flurry of excited chatter.

"This is Captain Martin speaking. We've encountered a bit of turbulence. Please remain seated, with seatbelts fastened, until we pass through the disturbance." Before Sarah had time to contemplate the inference of the "disturbance" interfering with their until-now-smooth flight, another flash of light clawed at the plane's tiny windows. A sudden shuddering of the aircraft's great silver body erased any question lingering in Sarah's mind. *This was an emergency*!

Once again, the captain's voice, laced with static, filled the cabin. "This is your captain speaking. Due to unstable weather conditions, we have encountered some unforeseen difficulties. It will be necessary for us to alter our flight plan. Our flight is being diverted to Atlanta. We will be landing shortly. Please, remain seated with seat belts fastened. Thank you."

An agitated buzz of frightened voices filled the tense air as passengers reacted to the pilot's unsettling announcement. Calm assurances from the stewardess did little to abate the undercurrent of alarm swirling through the cabin. Sarah could feel the hysteria crowding into her own chest, quickening the beat of her heart.

"Don't you worry none, little lady. We've got us a good pilot up there who knows what he's doing. There's no need for you to be afraid." The reassurance came from lips hovering near her ear.

Sarah turned her startled gaze toward the gray head bent close to her own; found herself looking into a pair of compassionate blue eyes; became aware of the tanned solicitous hand gently patting her knee.

*Oh, dear God.* What demented, hair-brained thinking prompted her to leave the comfort of her safe little apartment? Suddenly, the pettiness and mundane demands of the uneventful life she'd scoffed at less than a week ago, seemed far more appealing than being stuck at 35,000 feet aboard a distressed airplane, caught in the middle of a storm, facing the unwelcome advances of an aging Casanova.

"All seats must be in an upright position. Please, return your seats to their upright position."

Sarah welcomed the sharp directive delivered by the stern-faced stewardess making her way down the aisle. Quickly, Sarah's fingers jabbed the button on the arm of her chair, jolting her seat into its upright position while, at the same time, dislodging the unwelcome hand resting upon her knee. Smoothing her skirt over her lap, Sarah busied herself with the careful re-inspection of her seatbelt, purposely avoiding eye contact with the startled gentleman seated beside her. She was momentarily rescued from any further confrontation by the loud voice filling the plane with anger.

"Atlanta? We can't be landing in Atlanta. I have a plane to catch in Charleston at four o'clock." The outburst came from a young man seated across the aisle, his dark, handsome features distorted by rage.

The stewardess moved quickly to his side. "There is no need for concern, Sir. We will make every effort to be sure you arrive in time for your connecting flight."

"Well, you sure as hell better. I've got reservations in Ft Lauderdale tomorrow morning and I intend to be there."

Only slightly mollified, the young man's complaints subsided to muttered threats until, after what seemed an eternity of nervous uncertainty, the wheels of the aircraft gently kissed the concrete of the Atlanta runway.

There was an almost tangible air of uneasy restlessness as the passengers awaited further enlightenment from their pilot. It was several moments before his voice, once again, spit from the intercom. "We have encountered some mechanical difficulties which make it impossible to continue our flight as scheduled. Kindly gather your belongings and move into the terminal. Attendants will be available to assist you in arranging completion of your journey to your destination. We apologize for this inconvenience."

"Inconvenience?" The young man's anger rekindled. "What the hell kind of an airline is this? What about my connection out of Charleston?"

Once again the harried stewardess was at his side. "Sir, every effort will be made to assure you of making your connection."

"What the hell are we doing here in Atlanta, anyway? Just fix what's wrong with this pile of junk and let's get on our way."

"I'm afraid that isn't possible, Sir." Even from where she sat, it was obvious to Sarah the young woman was having difficulty containing her own anger. Sarah could only admire the display of such self-control.

"Well, you can be sure I'll not be flying with this airline again if this is the best service you can give me."

Apparently, the young man pushed one step beyond the attendant's endurance. Her next words sent chills shuddering across Sarah's shoulders. "For your information, Sir," the stewardess hissed, through tight lips. " That last bolt of lightening struck our aircraft. The plane's instrument panel has been damaged and until it is repaired, no one will be going anywhere on this plane."

+          +          +

Unfastening her seat belt, Sarah retrieved her carry-on, jammed beneath the seat in front of her, then rose hastily to her feet only to discover the here-to-fore unnoticed inadequacy of headroom. Forced to hunch awkwardly over the now empty aisle seat beside her, she waited as equally impatient passengers crowded into the limited space of the aisle. Having reluctantly endured assistance from her self-appointed traveling companion, who solicitously wrestled her luggage from the overhead compartment, Sarah wedged her way into the compressed crunch of humanity. Turning sideways, her coat scrunched beneath one arm, she inched her way along the narrow passageway, urging her suitcase ahead with one knee while her carryon, slung from her shoulder, bumped annoyingly at her derriere.

When at last she emerged from the plane's open doorway, it was to discover the disabled craft was being denied permission to snuggle up to one of the tunnels leading to terminal. Instead, the passengers were left with no alternative but to grope their way down a portable set of spindly metal stairs. Deliberately ignoring the tanned hand offering assistance at her elbow, Sarah tightened her fingers about the handle of her suitcase, stubbornly bounced the cumbersome piece of luggage across each narrow step, then grimly manhandled it across the uneven surface of the tarmac leading to the terminal.

More than a little flustered, not the least appeased by accommodating glass doors sliding gracefully open to grant her easy entry, Sarah allowed herself to be jostled along with the rest of the disgruntled clientele as they made their way to an apparently pre-designated ticket counter. Sarah frowned irritably at the row of smiling airline stewardesses awaiting them, looking so cool and poised in their freshly pressed uniforms, while she felt hot, disheveled and definitely out of sorts. Further undermining her rapidly disintegrating disposition, rudely crowded aside by impatient co-travelers, Sarah, to her chagrin, found herself positioned at the back of the line. There was nearly half an hour of frantic complaints, tearful supplications, and angry threats before a semblance of order was finally restored.

One harried young attendant stepped forward, her lips stretched into a tight, condescending smile.

"We do apologize for this inconvenience. Until other accommodations can be arranged, we'd like to offer you the comfort of the VIP lounge. We hope to have another plane available soon. We will notify you . . ."

"How long is that going to take?" This harsh demand came from the angry young man headed to Fort Lauderdale.

A bit of the forced congeniality seemed to slip from the attendant's fixed smile. "I'm sorry, Sir. I'm not exactly sure. Most of our aircraft are already in service. One will have to be brought in, but with this storm . . .."

"Look, I've got to be in Fort Lauderdale. You're gonna need to get me there on time or this airline's gonna be in a world of hurt."

"I assure you, Sir, every effort is being made to accommodate your connections. However, if you choose, you may wait-list yourself on stand-by for another flight. Or, if you wish to continue on down to Ground Transportation, arrangements are being made for buses to transport you closer to your destination. Otherwise . . ."

"Buses?" The incredulous gasp was more an expletive. Then, "Well, it's sure as hell better than hanging around here!" Muttering under his breath, the young man elbowed past Sarah, his long stride carrying him toward the directory sign to Ground Transportation.

"I'll help you to the lounge, little lady." Sarah glanced up into a now all-too-familiar pair of blue eyes, twinkling above the smile slashing its way beneath that neatly trimmed gray mustache. "We'll be more comfortable there."

*Well, that does it! I have no intention of sitting around some lounge, being "little ladyed" for the next . . . goodness knows how long.* Directing a puff of air from her lower lip in an attempt to dislodge the gray wisps of hair clinging to her damp forehead, Sarah lifted her chin and squared her shoulders "Thank you." She offered what she hoped would pass for a polite smile. "I believe I'll take the bus." With a toss of her head, she turned from her startled benefactor, his eyebrows arched in surprise, and stalked toward Ground Transportation, her bulging suitcase clacking across the tiled hallway as it wobbled obediently after her.

+        +        +

Sarah stared in confusion at the row of buses lining the curb. Now that she was outside the terminal, faced with a decidedly crucial decision, she realized the rashness of her actions. She had absolutely no idea which bus she should take, even if one would take her directly to Washington, D.C. where she was to join the tour group, or merely drop her off at some other airport. She scanned the lighted indicators announcing the affiliation of each bus. Nothing looked familiar.

Some of the vehicles sported tour banners across their sides; Brennan, Astro, Carnival. *What was the name of the tour group . . . didn't it begin with C?* She paused before the bus labeled "Carnival." *That seems vaguely familiar.*

Releasing her grip upon the handle of her luggage, Sarah plunged her hand into the overstuffed depths of her purse, groping among its multitudinous contents for her reservation documents. Then she remembered; thinking she'd not need them until she reached her destination, she'd packed them in her suitcase. With a sigh of annoyance, Sarah let her carry-on slip from her shoulders and dropped to her knees beside her bulging suitcase. Grasping its tasseled zipper, she urged the tiny teeth along their metal track, inwardly fretting over the unavoidable task of re-packing, as unruly items of confined wearing apparel eagerly leaped from their restrictive prison.

This irritant became secondary for Sarah as the hurried journey of the zipper was suddenly interrupted. Stopping at a point halfway to its destination, the little fastener refused to move forward or back, obviously having snagged upon the escaping sleeve of her cashmere sweater. Futilely, Sarah tugged at the stubborn clasp, but her efforts only succeeded in forcing the wool more tightly between the metal teeth. She searched her vocabulary for a word vile enough to express her anger. Tears of frustration stung her eyelids. What could she do now? In its present condition, she'd have no choice but to abandon her plan to check her suitcase for the balance of her flight. Yet how could she drag it around like this for the remainder of her journey, its cover half open, her clothes spilling out? Somehow, she'd have to repair it.

Having little other option available to her, Sarah slid the silk scarf from around her neck, wrapped it about the upper part of the baggage and, muttering dark incantations under her breath, jerked it irritably into a hard, merciless knot.

Thus involved, it was a moment before she noticed the pair of Nike sneakers planted beside her maimed piece of luggage; became aware of someone towering above her. Looking up, Sarah discovered the dark-haired young man from their aborted flight, apparently no longer angry, a disarming smile upon his lips.

"Looks like you're having a bit of trouble there." Leaning down, he placed his hand beneath her elbow. "Let me help you." He jerked his head toward the bus waiting at the curb in front of them. "This your bus?"

A little puzzled by his sudden change in attitude, Sarah allowed the young man to help her to her feet. "I …I think so," she stammered, glancing up nervously at the lighted destination indicator above the bus's front window. *Carnival . . .was that the name of her tour group?*

The young man's smile widened. "Hey, that's great. Here, let me help get your luggage aboard. Carnival sent this bus; it'll take us directly to the boat," he offered. "Nice to know somebody's looking out for us." Reaching down he scooped up the disabled suitcase, tucking it beneath his left arm before wrapping his fingers around the strap of her carry-on. "By the way," he grinned back over his shoulder. "My name is Eric. I expect we'll be seeing a lot of each other in the next few days."

A tiny gnat of uneasiness flitted about Sarah's subconscious as she followed Eric. *What was with this guy? Why the sudden congeniality? And what's this boat he's talking about?*

Pausing at the vehicle door, Eric stepped gallantly aside to allow Sarah to enter the bus ahead of him. She moved obligingly forward, one foot poised above the step, when her eyes fell upon the placard tucked into the bus's side window. "Welcome Cougars and Cubs." Somewhat tardily, but with searing clarity, an article she'd seen in last week's newspaper flashed across Sarah's memory, evoking an audible gasp from her lips.

"Carnival Cruise Lines hosts a Cougar/Cub Cruise. Designed especially for young men and older women," the header read.

*Oh dear God!* She released her hold on the door of the bus, stumbling backward into her young benefactor. "Oh, dear. I'm sorry, Eric," she stammered "I'm afraid there's been a terrible mistake. This isn't my bus after all."

The engaging smile froze on the young man's lips, the twinkling eyes of a moment before, turned cold, unfriendly. Hissing an uncomplimentary expletive, Eric dropped Sarah's mutilated luggage at her feet and, shoving rudely past her, pushed his way onto the bus.

Hastily reclaiming the handle of her discarded suitcase, Sarah slipped the strap of her carry-on over her shoulder, scurried back across the curb, along the sidewalk, and through the doors leading to Ground Transportation Operations.

"Excuse me," she murmured to the porter stepping forward to open the door for her. "Can you direct me to the VIP lounge?

+          +          +

Sarah hesitated before the formidable-looking portal, letting her eyes trace the letters of exclusion, *Red Carpet Lounge, Club Members Only* eloquently scrawled across its shiny red surface. With a twinge of discomfort, she envisioned the gathering of fellow passengers awaiting her inside and wished she could re-choreograph her recent flamboyant departure from their midst. For some reason, her power of recall chose that moment to replay the disbelief she'd seen in the face of the traveler with the gray mustache. The disturbing thought suddenly occurred to her; could he possibly have been aware of Eric's affiliation with the

Cougar/Cub cruise? That tiny gnat of annoyance flitted once again across her subconscious. *Then, why didn't he say something?* Annoyance escalated into irritation. *So help me, if he "Little Lady's" me one more time . . ..* A sigh escaped Sarah's lips. *Oh, well, there's no un-ringing the bell.*

Squaring her shoulders, Sarah took a deep breath and pushing open the door, stepped into the room. She quickly averted her eyes from the curious glances cast in her direction, but not before noting one pair of blue eyes; saw the gentleman's gray brows arch in surprise, then dip quickly in a frown of concern as his attention dropped to the pathetic bit of luggage following her. Perhaps it was the defiant set of her jaw that deterred him, or an inherent sense of compassion, but to Sarah's overwhelming relief, he did not rise to his feet to rush to her side.

Stoically, she made her way across the seemingly endless expanse of the room to a vacant table tucked unobtrusively in a far corner. Loosening her fingers from their death-like grip upon the suitcase handle, she let the strap of her carry-on slip from her shoulder. Dropping her purse onto the table, she flopped into the welcome comfort of the chair's soft cushion, suddenly surprised at how very tired she was—how terribly her arms ached. She stared down at the miserable-looking traveling bag cowering at her feet, the bright silk scarf restraining its bulging sides, the arm of her favorite sweater still imprisoned in the relentless teeth of the predatory zipper. The pink flannel of her nightgown peeked blatantly from an edge of the opening while the belt of her bathrobe, having inched its way through one unobstructed corner, now hung from the battered square of faux-leather like a bright blue chenille tail.

Realizing how ludicrous she must have looked tromping through the terminal, Sarah had a sudden irrepressible desire to laugh, felt the urge rising, gurgling within her chest. But when it reached her lips, it leaped forth, not in the form of mirth, but as one wrenching, uncontrollable sob. Quickly capturing the telltale gulps behind her hands, she closed her eyes and waited for the silent, unexpected shudders to pass through her exhausted body.

An almost inaudible click upon the tabletop, the uneasy awareness of another's presence, alerted Sarah she was no longer alone. Raising her eyes from the shelter of her fingertips, Sarah's startled gaze encountered a delicate tulip of glass resting on the table in front of her, a pale amber liquid sparkling from within. Her eyes darted to the now occupied chair across from her.

"I hope you don't mind if I join you, little lady." A suggestion of compassion toyed with the corners of a gentle smile slashing its way beneath the neatly-trimmed gray mustache. The gentleman raised the crystal container cradled in his own hand. "I hate drinking alone."

Sarah, her first reaction one of defensiveness, opened her mouth to offer a retort of reprimand for this invasion of her privacy. But some need rose inside her, the need for a sympathetic ally in this crumbling fiasco of her vacation, albeit it came in an offer of a tranquilizing sip of cool wine. She bit back the harsh words of angry reproach crowding to the back of her throat. Leaning forward, she wrapped her fingers about the stem of the wineglass and, lifting it to her lips, she smiled across its fragile rim.

"Thank you," Sarah murmured. "Thank you, very much."

+      +      +

"There, little lady, that ought to hold until you get to where you're going."

Somewhere, Sarah's new friend, whose name she learned was Alfred, managed to locate a role of duct tape.

"Yes, well, thank you, Alfred." Sarah skeptically eyed the unsightly mutation of faux leather bandaged in gray plastic, inwardly dreading the moment of claiming its ownership. Obviously, hers would not be the most attractive bit of luggage bumping along the baggage carousel, but at least her unmentionables, once again restrained, were no longer free to shamelessly flaunt themselves before the curious eyes of the traveling populace. Even more of a plus, she reminded herself, she now had the option of banishing this obnoxious bit of luggage to the baggage department.

As if reading her mind, Alfred's gaze followed hers to the mutilation that was her suitcase. "It is a pretty ugly piece, at that," he chuckled. "Well, we'll take it down to baggage and get it checked in," he offered, reaching for the handle of the bandaged bag. "The airline will see it gets on the right flight once we've been assigned another plane."

"That's very kind of you, Alfred," Sarah resisted. "But, really, I can manage."

"No problem, little lady," her benefactor assured her. "We'll pick up a new one when we get to D.C."

Whether it was the "we", or his knowledge of her destination causing her steps to falter, Sarah wasn't sure. "How—how did you know I was going to Washington, D.C.?"

"Sorry, I wasn't being nosey. Guess I noticed it on your boarding pass because that's where I'm headed. Fact is, I think we're signed up for the same tour."

"Really?" Sarah's voice sounded hollow even to her own ears.

"Best time of year to be in Washington—cherry trees'll be in full bloom. I think you're really going to enjoy this trip, little lady."

*Oh, dear, what was she getting herself into, a woman her age?* Comforting thoughts of the former predictability of her life scrambled across her mind: crafts on Tuesday, book club on Wednesday, bridge on Friday— with Alice.

*A woman her age—if there were no birthdays?* Sarah glanced toward a pair of blue eyes twinkling at her from above the soft canopy of a gray mustache.

"Yes." Her fingers strayed to the graying wisps of hair clinging limply to her forehead. "Yes," she smiled. "I do believe I am."

# TO DANCE IN THE RAIN

Like turtles, carrying our homes on our backs
We move through this all-too-short span of life.
Burdened by the flotsam and jetsam of our past,
Seeing things not as they are but as *we* are.

Compare me not with another you've known.
Let me prove myself for who and what I am,
Creating fresh new memories and not merely
Appendages to those from your past.

For I am a separate entity,
Nurturing my own love and admiration
For the wonder that is you,
And what your friendship means to me

I have not been where you have been,
Nor have you walked the paths I've known.
Yet in this special time that is ours
We can learn to dance in the rain